A Belief In Her

By

Barbara Valletto

ISBN 978-1-61929-489-9

Cover Design by AcornGraphics

Editors Nat Burns and Zee Ahmad

Publisher's Note:

Acknowledgments

As always, much thanks to Patty Schramm, Zee Ahmad, and Nat Burns for their outstanding guidance. Special thanks to all of my loved ones, who've been there from the start and continue to cheer me on.

Dedication

To our brave civilian and military forces who have fought, and continue to fight, in the name of peace and justice for all, you are not forgotten.

Special thanks to Patty Schramm for believing enough in me to create *A Belief in Her*.

Thank you so very, very much!

Chapter One

October, 1974

The military plane's flight to the southern coast of Vietnam was fraught with bone-jarring turbulence and sudden, drastic altitude drops. The nauseating smell of vomit, body odor, and nervous sweat threatened Claire McCallum's usually strong stomach. Unable to hold back, she surrendered to a bout of dry heaves that had her clutching an airsickness bag to her mouth and praying to God to put her out of her misery. She swore to herself that as soon as she got off the damn plane and stepped on solid ground, she'd drop to her knees and kiss the tarmac. When they finally did land, Claire gave a huge sigh of relief but nixed kissing the tarmac.

Sweltering heat struck her full in the face once she'd disembarked. Temperatures hovered in the mid-eighties, although humidity and the lack of a refreshing breeze made it feel much higher. When she tried to take a deep breath, she tasted sun-dried dirt.

Claire lined up with other passengers a short distance from the plane. If not for the other sole person of color standing among a group of white Americans, Claire would've stood out like a sore thumb. The occasional sidelong glance or double-take cast her way also didn't escape her notice. She sighed and ignored them. She hadn't journeyed to Vietnam to win friends or to make enemies.

A uniformed, middle-aged man walked up to their group. When the soldier beside her saluted, Claire reflexively followed suit, which made a few service personnel snicker. Smug bastards. Claire bit her tongue to stop herself from cursing under her breath.

"On behalf of the United States Air Force," the officer said, "I welcome you to Tan Son Nhut Air Base. Due to its complexity, TSN is made up of multiple sectors. Your deployment status will determine where you're housed on base. The military bus behind me will provide you with a guided tour en route to the proper sector."

The vehicle resembled a school bus that had been repainted a dull, putty gray. Its siding was splattered with mud and speckled with rust spots. A plume of black smoke belched from its rear exhaust pipe.

When its doors opened, a reed-thin officer with no military stripes hopped down. "Assignment papers, please."

Claire glanced at his name-tag, which read 'Dunfield,' and handed him a dog-eared packet.

"Claire McCallum," Dunfield said in a clipped tone. "American Red Cross. Interpreter. The ARC is stationed in Sector Ten, which is located the farthest from the air strip. Please step all the way to the rear of the bus and have a seat."

Before Claire could sidle past him, Dunfield yanked on her camera strap.

"Do you think you're on vacation, Recruit? If so, you're on the wrong base. For security reasons, photo taking is forbidden in most areas. It'd be wise to keep that in mind."

Claire gritted her teeth and fought down the urge to say, Keep your hands to yourself, asshole. Instead, she said, "Understood."

Gripping her satchel in one hand and readjusting her camera strap with the other, Claire moved to the back. One whiff had Claire tearing up and stifling a gag; the bus's noxious exhaust fumes were worse in the rear. Once all boarded, the bus jerked forward and Dunfield's voice crackled over the onboard PA system.

"Tan Son Nhut Air Base is the closest air base to Saigon and the busiest air base in the world. It serves as a vital location for all types of tactical and special operations. Our aircraft provide direct support and defensive action for our ground forces."

Through grimy windows, Claire watched the hustle and bustle of activity as uniformed personnel and civilians went about their everyday duties. Memories from a different time, a different era, flooded over her. Although the location was different, the sights and sounds were all too familiar and caused a pang of homesickness to settle in her chest.

She made a mental note to write to her parents once she settled in.

She gazed upon row after row of aircraft hangars and lots teeming with military vehicles.

Dunfield continued. "This strip consists of huge water towers, fuel stations, and silos housing military armaments and equipment. There's enough food and water housed in Sector Five for a six- to twelve-month stretch."

A pang of unease swirled in Claire's gut. If she had any doubts about the extent of the war effort, it was long gone now. This was the real deal. Claire's attention returned to the present when the bus came to a jarring stop.

"Sector Ten," Dunfield announced. "ARC personnel, please exit."

Claire and a handful of others grabbed their meager belongings and struggled up the narrow aisle. Claire mumbled gratitude to Dunfield before bounding down the steps and joining the other newcomers, who stood with eyes downcast, awaiting further instruction.

In Claire's opinion, ARC's sector seemed as unremarkable as the other housing sectors they'd passed. She assumed the four tented structures were sleeping quarters. Next to the tents stood a long row of wood-partitioned, outdoor showers. A discreet distance from the showers sat an outhouse building. Claire grimaced. So much for enjoying the pleasures of home. Now she knew why the ARC insisted on volunteers attending proper hygiene classes.

A plump, middle-aged woman, clad in a baby-blue tunic adorned with American Red Cross insignia patches, hurried toward the new arrivals. Tight blonde ringlets framed her full face and accentuated her seafoam-green eyes.

Smiling, the woman thrust out her hand to the closest volunteer and shook with him. "Hi. My name's Mary Kate Bunsen, and I'm your ARC liaison. I'm from Boise, Idaho, and have been part of the American Red Cross for close to ten years, five of those years stationed right here at Tan Son Nhut. On behalf of the American Red Cross, I welcome you to our team. Granted, it may not look like much, but looks are often deceiving."

One of the recruits sighed and wiped at his sweaty

brow. "My sentiments, recruit," Bunsen said. "You've arrived midway through the rainy season, where monsoons can crop up within a moment's notice and wreak hellish damage. It's best to be forewarned. You see the sky turn black, you run for shelter."

She swept the group with her gaze. "Some of you have signed on for six months of service or longer. Length of service isn't important. What *is* important is what each of you contributes to our universal humanitarian efforts abroad. As always, ARC is guided by seven fundamental principles. Can anyone name all seven?"

A scrawny male with a bad case of acne cleared his voice. "Humanity, neutrality, impartiality, independence, voluntary service, unity, and universality."

Mary Kate whooped with delight. "I couldn't have said it better myself. If we all hold true to these principles we will, indeed, make a difference in this world, and in this godforsaken war. Now—"

Mary Kate's words were cut off by the sound of music. Claire and the other volunteers turned to see a group of attractive young women lining up in a grassy field to the far right of the sleeping tents. As if on cue, they began dancing in unison and in rhythm to an upbeat tune.

"What's with the song and dance routine?" Claire asked.

Mary Kate's smile widened. "Oh, they're the Donut Dollies."

"Donut Dollies?"

"You know, they're the entertainment here on base. They do wonders to keep up our soldiers' morale."

On reflex, Claire reached for her camera bag but stopped short of opening its flap when she remembered Dunfield's earlier warning.

Bunsen must have noticed her hesitancy. "Oh, by all means take plenty of pictures while in our sector. Nothing is off limits here. Now, without further ado, my first task is to get you all situated. Males will occupy tent number two, and females tent number four. Bath stations are also segregated. Tonight is casual dress. Tomorrow, you'll be fitted for standard-issue uniforms such as what I'm wearing. Women will wear skirts and men, trousers. And boots. Toiletries, linens, and bath towels will also be provided. And plenty of pens and stationery." She moved her fingers as though checking things off. "Oh, entertainment! Television broadcasts are often a hit or miss and mostly reruns at that, but the base library's stocked for your reading pleasure, or if you need some alone time to clear your head."

Mary Kate tapped an index finger to her bottom lip. "Let's see. Am I missing anything? Oh, for goodness' sake. Food! You must be famished. The mess hall is cooking fried chicken, grits, and a mean apple cobbler that'll be served up within the hour. We'll have our meet and greet then. We share the mess hall with Medical Services personnel, so try not to dawdle or you may be left eating crumbs."

****

Tent four was huge, housing dozens of cots. Claire's stomach did another flip flop. Although thin cotton curtains separated the cots, they added little to no privacy.

Another ARC liaison handed Claire a pillow, a set of sheets, and a bag of toiletries. "Welcome. Cots are on a first come, first served basis, so take your pick. I suggest the far end, as it's closer to the bathroom and water fountains."

Taking her advice, Claire took the second-best location. Another recruit had beaten her to the first. A rusted metal locker and chipped hand mirror were the only additions to her sleep area. Claire scowled. What did she expect? A vase filled with fresh-cut flowers and a chocolate treat on her pillow?

She'd no sooner made her cot and put away her meager belongings when an overhead PA system announced chowtime.

In the short time it took for Claire to use the restroom, she ended up standing in a long line outside the mess tent, awaiting entrance. At the rate she was going, she'd be lucky if there were scraps left. She heard raucous laughter and looked ahead to see a group of female servicewomen exiting the tent. Damn. They must be Medical Services personnel. It looks like leftovers for me. One woman, in particular, caught her eye and made her heart skip a beat. Wow. What a looker. The woman's blonde hair had the texture of spun silk, and her skin was tanned and unblemished. She wore a baseball cap with the U.S. Air Force insignia. The top button on her shirt was undone, and her neck glistened with sweat. For a split second, their eyes made contact as she passed. Slate-gray eyes. How unusual.

"Better get a move on, Recruit," another woman said. "If you're lucky, you might get to gnaw on a drumstick."

Once inside the crowded mess tent, Claire hustled to the food line. The serving station reminded her of a school cafeteria. Claire picked up a plastic tray and moved along to the plates, napkins, and cutlery table.

Apron-tied ARC cooks greeted hungry recruits with smiles and, to Claire's surprise, loaded a hefty portion of fried chicken wings onto her plate. This time, there were no uncomfortable stares or nervous smiles. Claire felt as if she was treated the same as all the other recruits and it felt good. Damn good. She hit the refreshment counter last and snagged a lukewarm bottle of Pepsi before finding a seat at a long picnic bench in a far corner. Six of the eight volunteers who rode the bus with her earlier were already seated. Claire glanced about the room, looking for the other sole person of color from the bus ride. He wasn't there and she wondered if jet lag had gotten the best of him. The acne-scarred recruit smiled at her and inched over. Claire had no sooner sat down when Mary Kate hip-checked her on the bench to allow more room for her ample derriere.

Mary Kate smiled and bobbed her head as if it were connected to her neck with springs. "My, my, you all sure clean up well. I can't wait to see you in your official ARC uniforms. I have a feeling you're going to make me proud during your stay here."

Mary Kate eyed her plate and made a show of licking her burgundy-tinted lips and rubbing her ample belly. "Yummy. Nothing like Southern fare to make you feel all warm and cozy. And wait until you taste dessert. It'll knock your socks off."

Claire stifled a laugh. Southern fare, meaning fried delights in American cuisine, could never hold a candle to

Vietnamese Southern fare and its plethora of delicacies. In this heat, Claire would've preferred a nice chilled cucumber salad with all the fixings.

Mary Kate leaned forward so she could address the group. "Please, don't hesitate to dig in. We wouldn't want your food to get cold. I must say, I'm tickled pink to hear each of your life stories, and how you decided to devote yourself to helping the needy. Let's start with you, sweetie, with that shock of red hair and adorable spattering of cheek freckles."

The female recruit cringed at the sudden attention. "My name's Quincy," she said in a meek voice. "I'm from Jersey City, New Jersey."

"Hello, Quincy from Jersey City, New Jersey! What appealed to you most about joining the Red Cross?"

Claire smirked. Mary Kate sounded like an overzealous game show host.

Quincy squirmed in her seat. "My mom performed with the USO during WWII. She said her time abroad shaped her into the responsible, independent woman she is today."

"USO, huh? There might be an opening for you in entertainment."

Mary Kate glanced at her roster and moved on to the next recruit. And on to the next. And the next. Claire learned that most came from rural areas as opposed to big cities. For three recruits, college was in their future. The others claimed that their ARC stint offered them a last opportunity to live free before life and all its demands forced them to grow up. When it was Claire's turn, Mary Kate asked. "Claire McCallum? From Hobarth, New York. Such an Americanized name for one, I assume, is native to this area."

Claire stifled the urge to roll her eyes. Did it ever end? In as neutral a tone as she could muster, she said, "Yes. I'm of Vietnamese origin but immigrated to the states when I was a child."

"Delightful. I assume adapting to a totally different culture must've been a challenge."

Claire shrugged. "I survived."

"I see. And how, my dear, do you intend to serve?"

"As an interpreter. It's my hope that I can help ease the language barrier between the Vietnamese people and our team."

"And the camera?"

"I want to capture all aspects of this war. Not just the humanitarian efforts."

Mary Kate blinked. "I'm not sure I understand what you mean, dear. There are restrictions as to where you can take photos."

"I realize that, but I'm hoping an opportunity will arise to expand my horizons."

"In what way?"

"Maybe accompany a unit on patrol."

Mary Kate scoffed. "You mean in the battlefield? That's unheard of. You're a civilian. You're not permitted in any area where your life may be in danger. Your role as interpreter is solely base specific."

"But our country deserves to see the true Vietnam, the uncensored version."

Mary Kate's complexion turned almost as red as her lipstick. It took the woman a few moments to respond. "Well, Claire McCallum, may God's grace protect you on your true chosen path. For now, though, you are to report to the Medical Services Unit at 8:00 a.m. tomorrow. Your direct report is Captain Calder. The captain will explain all duties expected of you then. Now, to the rest of you..." Mary Kate continued handing out assignments while avoiding making any eye contact with Claire.

Dessert was a banana split, instead of the cobbler. Claire ate it as quickly as she could, then excused herself and retired to her sleeping quarters. Cursing under her breath in Vietnamese, she kicked off her sandals, pulled off her Grateful Dead T-shirt, and wriggled out of her faded bellbottoms. Bunsen doesn't know diddly squat. There must be ways for her to sneak off base, under the radar, to explore. Has to be. And she'd damn well find it.

In the moments before Claire drifted off to sleep, she remembered the blonde-haired woman exiting the mess tent, and smiled in spite of her frustration.

Chapter Two

At eight a.m. sharp, Claire entered the Medical Services Unit, which was housed in a huge plane hangar. For the umpteenth time, she pulled at the stiff collar of her ARC uniform. She hated having to button up to the neck. In this weather, she was sure to get prickly heat.

Uncertain where to go, Claire touched the arm of the closest military person. She quickly glanced at his nametag: Sgt. Salvatore. "Excuse me, Sergeant. Can you please direct me to Captain Calder's office?"

He smiled. "You're in luck. I'm Captain Calder's aide. And you are?"

"ARC recruit Claire McCallum. I'm here in an interpreter capacity, but I'm kind of a Jane of all Trades, so wherever I'm needed, count on me being there."

Salvatore grinned. "Thank God for that. We've been waiting weeks. If you'll follow me, I'll escort you to the captain's office."

Calder's office was partitioned off from the main area with plywood panels. Furniture was limited to a pitted metal desk, file cabinet, and two chairs. A manual typewriter sat on the desk's edge.

Right as Salvatore motioned for Claire to sit in the chair opposite the desk, his walkie-talkie came to life, full of high-volume static.

"Excuse me one minute," Salvatore said. From the hallway, Claire heard a short, garbled conversation. Salvatore returned and said, "I hate to inform you that Captain Calder's been called away to a staff meeting. I'm not sure how long the meeting will go."

"It's okay. I can wait."

Salvatore stroked his clean-shaven chin. "While you wait, would you be willing to help out in another capacity?"

"Absolutely. Name it."

"We're short a clerical assistant. How are your typing skills?"

"On average, sixty words a minute with zero typos."

"God, that's good news! I'm a two finger pecker, at best."

Salvatore opened a file cabinet drawer, pulled out a brown manila folder, and handed it to Claire.

"Here's a bunch of purchase orders that need processing. If you can get through at least the first ten, that'd be a tremendous help."

"Consider it done."

"Much obliged, ARC Recruit McCallum." Salvatore did a mock salute and left.

Claire traded chairs so she now sat behind Captain Calder's desk. She reached for a PO form and slid it into the typewriter roll. She then opened the file and set to work. Most files were easy to read but twenty minutes later, she hit her first road block. Claire squinted at the scrawled notations on a supply order. "What a bunch of chicken scratch," she muttered.

"Excuse me?"

Claire's head whipped up to find a striking vision: a woman dressed in an olive-colored T-shirt and fatigue pants staring at her with slate-gray eyes and a smirk on her full lips.

Oh, my God. Oh, my God. Oh, my God. It's her. The woman coming out of the mess tent last night. The one with those incredible eyes.

Claire swallowed the imaginary lump in her throat and croaked, "Can I help you?"

"I imagine you could, if you'd be able to decipher my, what did you call it? Chicken scratch?"

Burning heat flared up from Claire's core and seared her cheeks. If there had been a rock big enough, she would've burrowed a hole beneath it and stayed put until the world failed to exist. Tongue-tied, she watched the woman lean down and pluck the supply order from her clammy hands.

The woman frowned. "Yes, I do have to admit that my writing could be a bit challenging." She handed Claire a lined notepad. "Let's try this again with my dictating. Allow me to help you decipher."

Claire grabbed a fresh order form.

"I'll need ten cartons of gauze bandages—the ten-by-ten size. Any smaller wouldn't serve our injured troops' needs more than a box of kiddie bandages. I'll need three cases each of splints, slings, Betadine, and rubber tubing for IV use." The woman hesitated for a brief moment. "Are you getting this, or am I going too fast?"

"Um. Yes."

"Yes, you're getting this? Or yes, I'm going too fast?"

"Yes, I'm getting this."

"I want you to put in a separate request to the Red Cross for plasma and the following blood types." Claire flipped to a fresh page and scribbled to keep up.

Once finished, the woman asked, "Is there anything else you need?"

"Your name, please," Claire said.

The woman arched a brow. "Do you want my rank and serial number as well?"

"If you wouldn't mind, yes. Except for the serial number. I don't think that's necessary."

"I'm Captain Margaret Anne Calder, United States Air Force. That's Anne with an *e*."

Claire felt the blood drain from her face. Busted. Calder glanced at Claire's order pad. "Now, look whose writing resembles chicken scratch."

****

Captain Margaret Anne Calder with an *e*'s supply request was one of fifty requests Claire processed her first day on base. As for Calder, Claire didn't see hide nor hair of her for the rest of the day. Maybe it was best they kept their distance. It would give Claire time to think of a way to set things right after putting her foot in her mouth the first damn day on the job.

At the end of her work day, Claire walked the mile trek to ARC's sector. She stopped in the mess hall for a quick bowl of chili and a slice of corn bread before retiring for the night. She groaned when she eyed the stationery pad and pen sitting on top of her locker.

An inner voice urged: The letter isn't going to write itself, McCallum. The longer you stall, the longer it's going to take for hurt feelings to heal. It's best to get it over with.

Claire snatched the pad and pencil and sat cross-legged on her lumpy mattress. Under the dim glow of an overhead emergency light, Claire put pen to paper.

Dear Mom and Dad,

Please don't hate me.

She cursed and scratched out the line about hating. Talk about dramatic. She started again.

I understand that my actions have caused you great pain.

Yes, yes. That's it. Acknowledge that she'd hurt them, but don't apologize. No 'buts' in this letter.

Life has taken a new course for me. I've long known that my involvement with the war is not best served at home, but rather in the midst of the turmoil. Much as you both served with the American Red Cross abroad in years past, especially working with displaced persons, I choose to do the same.

Although following in your footsteps might not be your desire for me, it's become a need to be involved in any way possible in order to make a difference. It is my hope that, with time, you will come to understand and accept my wishes.

Love, Claire

There. Done. Short, but sweet. Give them time to take it all in. Try to again convince them that Vietnam is where I need to be. That I'll be serving both America and Vietnam in a way I've always dreamed of but never had the opportunity to pursue. Until now.

She folded the letter, slid it into an envelope, and placed

it on top of her locker. First thing in the morning, she would drop it over at Postal Services. She quickly undressed and slid beneath a thin sheet. In the moments leading up to sleep, Claire's thoughts centered on Calder and how her deep gray eyes reminded her of storm clouds brewing.

Chapter Three

After a restless night's sleep, Claire awoke foggy-headed and irritable. Just the thought of seeing Captain Calder made her sick to her stomach. She had to find a way to make amends, even if it meant walking right up to her, collapsing at her feet, and begging forgiveness.

Wanting to at least eat something, Claire popped into the mess tent to snag a plain, untoasted bagel before dropping her letter to her parents at Postal Services and moving on to Medical Services.

Claire eyed a row of bikes leaning on kickstands beside a low retaining wall and considered signing one out. Nah. Best to walk. It'd give her more time to clear her head.

The closer Claire came to the MSU hangar, the more sluggish her movements became, as if her feet were encased in cement. She felt like a prisoner walking to her execution. She hated to admit it, but she was scared senseless Calder was still pissed off about yesterday.

A shrill whistle sounded, stopping her in her tracks. She turned and saw Salvatore waving at her.

"Hey, Claire. We're over in the map room. Care to join us?"

Us. Plural. Claire's tension eased ever the slightest. Well, at least she wouldn't be left alone with Calder and at her mercy.

After a series of twists and turns, Claire came face-to-face with Calder. And her heart pounded out a staccato beat. Calder was clad in a white T-shirt and olive-colored khakis. Capless, her hair hung loose and framed her face in a bob style. She was leaning over a large regional map, red-penciling an area in the map's lower right corner.

"Captain Calder," Salvatore said. "I'd like to introduce you to Claire McCallum. She's with the ARC. She's fluent in Vietnamese and a damn good typist. Yesterday, she knocked out a shi...I mean, a stack of purchase orders for us."

Calder dropped the pencil onto the table and looked up. When her eyes met Claire's, Claire swore she saw a hint of a smile on her lips.

"Yes, Sergeant. Chicken Scratch and I have already met, if only briefly."

Salvatore scratched his head. "Chicken Scratch?"

Calder laughed. "Personal joke, Sergeant. Thanks for your help. That's all for now."

Salvatore shrugged, saluted, and left.

Once alone, the tension became so thick Claire imagined it could be cut with a knife. *Or maybe I'm imagining things. From the look on Calder's face, she seems more amused by me than annoyed.*

"I'm glad to see that you came back," Calder said.

Claire nodded.

Calder motioned to a chair. "Please, have a seat." She opened a blue folder. "Claire McCallum. ARC Recruit. Interpreter position. Hometown: Hobarth, New York."

"Yes."

Claire braced herself for the onslaught of questions about how a Vietnamese woman ended up stateside and was surprised when she noticed that Calder hadn't even batted an eye.

Instead, Calder extended her hand. "On behalf of the United States Air Force, welcome to Vietnam."

Claire shook Calder's hand and let out a nervous giggle. The heat of her skin felt electric.

"I'm sorry. Did I say something funny?" Calder asked.

"Oh, no. Not at all, Captain Calder. It's just that..." Claire stopped herself. *How could she explain that she was expecting to be grilled about race and ethnicity, only to have it not mentioned at all? At least, so far.*

Calder arched a brow.

"It's nothing," Claire said.

"Hmm." Calder again glanced at Claire's folder.

"You're a photography major."

"Yes."

"Interesting. Photojournalism is a worthy profession."

"It's my hope to gain some exposure out in the field."

"As in battlefield?"

Claire nodded.

"Not too sure about that, Chicken Scratch, but you have to start somewhere. Maybe, with enough experience, you'll get your wish."

The more they talked, the more the tension in Claire's neck and shoulders eased. This wasn't bad at all. Maybe the worst was over.

Calder closed the folder and clasped her fingers on the desk in front of her.

"I ask all new recruits who work for me the same two questions. Why are you really here, and what's motivated you to come all this way? Before you answer, I must tell you that you'd be surprised how many recruits respond with the answer of acting on a misguided whim."

The hairs on the nape of Claire's neck bristled. "That is certainly not the case for me, Captain Calder. During spring break from college, I came home one night to find my parents watching a TV news broadcast of a South Vietnamese fishing village that had been attacked by the Viet Cong and burned to the ground. At first, I couldn't comprehend what I was seeing. The bodies... the fire, it all seemed so surreal. Those images haunted me for months. I mean, those victims were civilians living a peaceful existence, much like me and my brother, Minh—"

Calder's eyes widened. "You have a brother?"

Claire bit her tongue. Shut up. Shut up. Shut up. "Had, Captain."

"Oh. Do you want to talk about it?"

Claire wiped a sheen of sweat from her forehead. "Maybe some other time."

"So, you're originally from Vietnam?"

Claire nodded. Here it comes. "My American parents worked for the ARC in Vietnam prior to the war heating up. As I was orphaned at birth, they adopted me, and took me back to live in the states."

This time, when Calder looked at her, there was a softness to her face. Was it pity lurking in her eyes, or a silent understanding? Too hard to tell.

"I apologize for interrupting. Please, go on," Calder said.

Claire took a deep breath. "Anyway, after graduation, I joined the anti-war movement and fought for peace efforts abroad. I participated in rallies, sit-downs, and fundraisers. I pounded the pavements handing out flyers and hanging up pro-peace posters. I appealed to state reps and congressman. Before long, though, I became dissatisfied that my efforts weren't making any difference at all. So, I joined the ARC as an interpreter and here I am."

"And your parents? How did they take the news of your returning to Vietnam?"

"Not good at all. My mother reacted with fits of hysterics, and my father with a detached resignation. He wanted to know what I was trying to prove. I insisted I wasn't out to prove anything, only that I felt compelled to make a difference, no matter how small or inconsequential it may be. It didn't help matters that I dropped the bombshell within hours of leaving, and then took off in the middle of the night before they had a chance to talk me out of it."

Calder winced. "Ouch."

Claire grimaced. "Yeah. Talk about screwing up royally. I'm hoping a letter I sent might smooth things over."

Calder leaned back and placed her hands behind her head. "Well, in any event, you're here with or without your parents' blessing. I, for one, am pleased to welcome you to Tan Son Nhut and look forward to working with you. As I have a full agenda, I'm dismissing you for the remainder of the day. Rest up, though, because tomorrow at noon, we'll roll up our sleeves and get to work. I hope you don't mind getting your hands dirty."

"Not at all, Captain."

"Good. Because all facets of war are dirty. From here on out, your life will revolve around following my orders, and my orders alone. Do I make myself clear?"

"Yes."

"Yes, what?"

"Yes, Captain Calder."

"Dismissed."

****

Back in ARC's sector, Claire changed into a pair of jeans, T-shirt, and sandals before snagging her camera and hitting the mess tent for a soggy grilled cheese sandwich and lukewarm bowl of tomato soup. Looking down at the bland meal made her thoughts swirl with memories of home and her mother's exceptional cooking talents. Not only had her mother introduced her to American cuisine, but she'd made a concerted effort to recreate authentic Vietnamese fare, so Claire could remain in touch with her roots. Her mother had also gone the extra mile in connecting Claire with children who shared her cultural heritage so that she would never lose sight of who she was or where she came from.

As she meandered about the base, she took in her surroundings with a keen eye for detail. Many service personnel were aiding injured soldiers either by pushing their wheelchairs or flanking them as they hobbled with canes. Jeeps whizzed by, carrying boxes of supplies. Claire chuckled at a speeding Jeep being chased by a horn-blasting MP cop. Twenty yards ahead, a group of Donut Dollies were practicing a dance routine in a grassy area, and Claire didn't hesitate to take aim, focus, and shoot an array of photos.

Next stop in her travels had her passing by a gaming tent, where a heated ping-pong tournament was underway. She peeked in, espied Quincy leaning against a partitioned wall on the opposite side of the room, and decided to join her.

"Hi," Claire said.

Quincy cracked a thin smile and edged aside to give Claire room.

"Why aren't you practicing with the Glam Gals?" Claire asked.

"Glam Gals?"

"The Dollies. It's my nickname for them."

"Didn't feel up to it. I have period cramps."

"Oh." Claire mentally calculated when her period was due. Two weeks. Ugh.

"It's so damn hot here, I've already taken three showers today," Quincy moaned.

"I feel your pain."

Claire eyed two elderly men using mini rackets to volley a white, lightweight ball from one end of a long table to the other, with a net separating the table midway. Both men were sweating from exertion and swearing like drunken sailors depending on who held the lead at any given moment.

Claire whistled. "They look like they're out for blood."

"Stakes are high."

"How high?" Claire asked.

"The loser has to fork over one hundred bucks and a bottle of Jack Daniels."

"No wonder they're so competitive. Kind of old to be in the military, aren't they? They both look like they're in their late sixties."

Quincy shrugged. "Maybe they're civilian."

"Maybe."

Instinctively, Claire reached for her camera.

Quincy gripped her hand. "I wouldn't do that if I were you."

"Why?"

"If a flash goes off and messes up this match, your ass will be grass."

Claire grimaced. "Damn, another missed moment. I would've loved to have captured their expressions. Their intensity."

In comfortable silence, Claire and Quincy watched the game play out for close to an hour until a vicious paddle slam clinched the game. The winner roared in triumph and the loser cursed in defeat.

While the small crowd of onlookers dispersed, Claire and Quincy helped themselves to ice-cold bottles of Fresca out of a large Styrofoam cooler. Claire popped its cap, closed her eyes, and took a long swig. In that moment she imagined sitting on her front porch at home, soaking up the rays of a late summer sun.

A sharp nudge in her side made her scowl. "What did you do that for, Quincy?"

"You totally zoned out."

Claire shrugged. "Just thinking about home."

"Yeah. Me, too. Do you ever have second thoughts about coming here?" Quincy asked.

"Never. Vietnam was once my home. Seeing it now, so battle ravaged, makes me sick to my stomach and further strengthens my need to help."

"Yeah. I get it."

Claire sensed that Quincy wanted to say something further.

"What?" Claire asked.

Quincy squirmed. "Nothing."

"Seriously, Quincy. What do you want to ask me?"

"I was wondering if, considering your ethnicity, do you ever feel torn between two worlds? Two Vietnamese worlds. The North and the South? I mean, these are all your people."

Claire contemplated Quincy's question for a moment before answering. "They are. And each side believes the other is right in fighting for their beliefs. I'm from South Vietnam, so it makes it that much harder to come to terms with the fighting and victimization from the North. It's so different in the states. So free and liberating."

"Life, liberty, and the pursuit of happiness, right?" Quincy scoffed.

"Why the sarcasm?"

"The U.S. is a far cry from the land of the free and the home of the brave, that's for sure. Its history is rife with its own atrocities."

Claire looked down and noticed one of her shoelaces was untied. "I guess."

Quincy sighed and glanced at her watch. "Enough with the heavy talk. We better get a move on or Buns will be up our asses for missing curfew."

Once in the sleeping tent, Claire changed into a sleeveless T-shirt and boxer shorts, and nestled beneath the sheet. She replayed the day's events in her mind. Although much had transpired, Claire couldn't get Calder's image out of her mind. Her eyes. Her lips. How she so wanted to kiss them. How she so wanted to... Oh, never mind. The reality of locking lips with Calder was as much a fat chance as taking photos in the battlefield. Two lost causes. Did it get any worse than that?

Lulled by the overhead fan dispersing heated air within the stuffy tent, Claire drifted into a dreamless slumber.

Chapter Four

Claire awoke at the break of dawn. Eager to begin her day, she'd showered, straightened up her sleeping area, and ate a full breakfast by eight. For the umpteenth time, she glanced at her wristwatch and groaned. Four more hours to go before she could head to Medical Services. How should she spend the time?

As soon as the thought surfaced, Mary Kate Bunsen popped her head into the sleeping tent and crooked her finger at Claire. "Recruit McCallum? I wonder if you could assist me."

Although assisting Bunsen wasn't on her to-do list, Claire forced a smile. "Of course."

"Communications has a bunch of audio-taped enemy intel that needs translating. Are you up to the task?"

Claire's smile widened at an opportunity to use her skills. "I'd be happy to."

"Excellent. It shouldn't take you more than an hour or two."

"Sure thing."

An hour later, Claire removed her headphones and switched off a compact tape recorder. She looked down at her written translations and grimaced. Most of the taped recording was garbled to the point where accurate deciphering was near impossible. Although reassured by Communications that every little bit helped, Claire didn't feel as optimistic.

She looked at her watch. Ten-thirty. There was still time to kill. Claire found Quincy setting up folding tables and chairs in a small tent enclosure. "Hey, Quincy! What are you up to?"

"Assisting the injured with writing letters to loved ones back home. Do you want to help?"

That's what Claire was talking about. Doing something for the needy. Making a fucking difference. "Sure thing."

Ten minutes later, Quincy motioned for the first soldier in line to enter, and Claire motioned to the second.

One look at the scowl on the soldier's face was all it took for Claire to realize he hadn't expected a Vietnamese woman to help him with writing a letter home. Damn, just when she thought things might be looking up.

She watched a young, scrawny soldier with his scalp and right side of his face wrapped in gauze, nudge the soldier forward. The soldier didn't budge.

"What the hell's wrong with you, man?" the scrawny soldier asked.

"I ain't too keen on this arrangement," the other grumbled.

"Then step aside, dude. Daylight's wasting."

With a grunt, the soldier stormed out of the tent and the injured one shuffled forward and took a seat opposite her. Up close, she saw that his exposed eye was teary and bloodshot.

"Good morning. I'm ARC Recruit Claire McCallum at your service. Your name, please."

"First Lieutenant Roy Somerfield."

"Who would you like to write to today, Lieutenant?"

"My fiancée, Ruth. She—We live in Spokane, Washington." The soldier bounced his knees up and down as if they were on springs. The table shuddered from the impact.

"There's no need to be nervous, Lieutenant," Claire said. "I'm here to help."

"The thing is, I'm not sure how Ruth's going to react to what I have to tell her. But I want her to be prepared before I'm honorably discharged and we meet face-to-face. I want her to have time to adjust."

"You mean to your injury?"

Somerfield nodded.

"I'm more than willing to lend a sympathetic ear, but I must tell you that the military restricts going into detail about anything that happens in the field or on base in written correspondence."

"So we have to sugarcoat everything, right?"

Claire nodded. "I'm sorry."

Somerfield sighed. "It sure as hell couldn't hurt. While

on patrol on the outskirts of a paddy field I got caught up in a napalm attack. Something about coordinates being skewed and my being in the wrong place at the wrong time. Doctors don't hold out much hope of me ever getting my sight back in my one eye. And then, there's the problem with my scalp, and the hair follicle damage."

"You're alive. That's what's important."

Roy sniffed. "I know. I'm lucky a reconnaissance chopper saw me and flew me back to base. Some members of my unit weren't near as lucky."

Touched to the core by the soldier's bravery, Claire resisted the urge to hug him. "You should be proud that you've served your country and lived to tell the tale. Believe you me, the fact that you're not returning to the States in a flag-draped casket will have Ruth thanking the heavens above."

A lone tear slid down Roy's cheek and Claire whipped out a tissue and handed it to him. "But what if she doesn't want to marry me? What if she's repulsed by me?"

"There's one thing that I truly believe in and that's love's ability to endure any challenge, any hardship, and still remain strong. You have to remain strong, Lieutenant, and hold fast to the belief that what you and Ruth share is genuine."

Roy met her eyes. "You're sure?"

"Dead sure. Shall we begin?"

Dear Ruth,

As presently I am unable to write on my own, an ARC recruit is writing for me. I cannot go into much detail but to say that I have suffered an injury and I will be coming home sooner than expected. Please do not spend any time worrying about me. I am in good spirits and so looking forward to our upcoming nuptials and our future together.

Much love and adoration,
Ray

Claire folded the letter and slid it into an envelope.

"You did great, Lieutenant. All I need now is your fiancés address, and I'll get this right in the mail."

When Roy stood to leave, Claire grabbed his hand and shook it. "Thank you for your service, Lieutenant. Thank you so very much."

Roy lips quivered. "You're a godsend, Miss McCallum. Thank you."

Over the following hour, Claire assisted three additional injured soldiers with writing home. Their tales shocked yet intrigued her. Often, Claire blinked back tears and swallowed her outrage. Her fingers ached from holding the pen too tight. But, despite it all, Claire felt honored to be part of listening to the soldiers' stories and decided she'd assist Quincy with letter-writing duty any chance she could.

When finished, Quincy collected eight sealed envelopes and wrapped the thick bundle in an elastic band. "Claire, would you mind dropping these off at Postal Services? I can't ditch dance practice two days in a row without Bunsen having a cow."

Despite a change of scenery and some much-needed fresh air, Claire felt as if she carried the weight of the world on her shoulders. Listening to the soldiers' gruesome war accounts of battles won and lost, lives taken and saved, tore at her emotions. Now she knew how Atlas must've felt.

Claire no sooner left the post office when a familiar face appeared—the man who had won the ping-pong tournament the night before. For the first time, she noticed he walked with a severe limp.

"Hey!" Claire shouted.

The man stopped and turned. "Do I know you, little lady?"

"Nope, but I know you. You're the guy from last night's game, the one with the mean-handed smash."

The man grinned and puffed out his chest. "I am one and the same. And you might be…"

Claire covered the distance between them in two long strides and observed his craggy appearance in better detail. His eyes were a faded blue, with a thin white film clouding the right eye. His hair was pure white, cut in a modified crewcut style. His hands were heavily veined and gnarled.

Although slight in build, Claire sensed he had once been a strong man. "Claire McCallum. I'm an interpreter with the Red Cross."

The man extended his hand. "I'm Staff Sergeant George Waldron. Retired staff sergeant, that is. It's a pleasure to meet you, Miss McCallum."

"Oh, the pleasure's all mine. It's not every day a gal gets to meet Tan Son Nhut's reigning ping-pong champion."

George chortled. "Flattery will get you everywhere, my dear. Where are you headed?"

"Medical Services."

"Oh, you must be helping out Captain Calder and her crew."

"Yes."

"She runs a tight ship, that Calder. The all business, no pleasure type."

"No kidding."

George continued. "She's made quite a few enemies on base, but that's beside the point. I, myself, like her. She's got guts, and she's as smart as a whip."

"Uh-huh." Claire changed the subject. "So, is a ping pong rematch in the works?"

George laughed so hard, he coughed. "I whupped Dickey's butt so bad, it'll be a cold day in hell if he has the guts to challenge me again."

Claire glanced down at her watch.

George followed her gaze. "Oh, my apologies, missy. Far be it from me to keep you from your duties."

"Sorry, but I'd hate to be late on my first day. Well, second, actually."

"Nor should you." George again thrust out a hand. "For the record, though, I'm damned pleased to make your acquaintance, Claire McCallum."

"The feeling's mutual, Retired Staff Sergeant George Waldron."

George tipped his service cap and hobbled off.

****

Now familiar with MSU's layout, Claire went straight

to Calder's office and knocked.

"Come in." A voice sounded from within.

Claire turned the knob and entered. And stifled a gasp. There sat Captain Calder in all of her radiant beauty, dressed in full USAF uniform.

Claire cleared her throat. "Good morning, Captain Calder."

Calder surprised her with a broad smile. "Indeed it is, ARC Recruit McCallum. Ready to get started?"

So much for small talk, Claire thought, moving toward a chair.

"Oh, no time for sitting, McCallum. We hit the ground running. You are trained in first aid, right?"

"Yes. And CPR."

"Excellent. Medical Services is a triage unit, which means injured soldiers are brought here for treatment. At one time or another, you may be needed to assist me or a surgeon in our OR."

Claire blinked. "Are you a doctor?"

"Registered nurse."

"Captain, are all injured ground troops transported to Tan Son Nhut?" Claire asked.

"Depends on their location. Tan Son Nhut is one of many triage bases. The severity of a soldier's injuries determines if he or she is either airlifted off base to a trauma hospital on the mainland, or treated here and allowed adequate recuperation time before rejoining their company. There are also U.S. hospital ships situated all along the South China Sea that are equipped to receive and treat the injured transported by helicopter. MSU is not only responsible for tending to the injured, but with working closely with the Aerial Logistics Department in mapping out coordinates for chopper drop-offs of food, water, and medical supplies to ground units. I need to forewarn you from the start that most days, working here is demanding and stressful."

"I'm up for the challenge."

"Glad to hear it. Today, thank God, there are no surgeries scheduled, but there's plenty of follow-up patient care needed. Blood pressure monitoring, wound cleansing, meds dispensement, and the occasional resuture if stitches have

opened up. Grab that med kit over there and a gown and follow me. You're going to be my shadow."

Claire felt as if she'd gone from treading atop smoldering embers to being directly thrown into a roaring flame.
The patient list was huge and treatment unique to each
affected person. As Calder had warned, Claire saw much
blood, gore, infection and the like as they made their
rounds. Out of the corner of her eye, she noticed one of the
Donut Dollies holding an injured soldier's hand and wiping
sweat from his brow.

"What's going on over there?" Claire asked.

Calder looked over and frowned. "He's probably suffering from PTSD and needs some TLC."

"I get it. I don't know how our soldiers do what they do
day in and day out. Earlier, I helped an injured soldier write
a letter home to his fiancé. He told me about how he had
been injured. If a heart can ever bleed with sympathy, mine
did."

Calder nodded. "In this environment, it's tough to let
things go, but you have to or you'll be dragged down with
despair."

"Any words from the wise?"

"It may sound insane, but I'm the deep-breath-taking
type."

"Which is?"

"For each breath in, I absorb a soldier's pain. For each
breath out, I release the pain. I imagine that during that brief
moment, a soldier is at peace."

For just an instant, Claire saw true emotion on Calder's
face and realized that Calder wasn't as much of a hard ass as
she made herself out to be.

For the remainder of the day, they silently worked side
by side, focused on each patient's needs. When it reached
the dinner hour, they disposed of their nitrile gloves and
gowns before returning to Calder's office.

"Wow. We sure had ourselves one chaotic day," Calder
said. "Time to call it quits, McCallum."

Claire sagged into a chair. "Amen to that."

"I must admit, I'm impressed with your skills and the
way you took on every situation with care and attention to

detail. We really had our groove going on, didn't we?"

Claire smiled at the comment. "We sure did. I don't know what hurts worse, the burning in my feet from standing all day, or the finger cramps from updating charts."

Calder chuckled. "I hear you. Sometimes the pace around here is nonstop. I see a hot bath in the near future to ease my sore muscles."

Claire grimaced. Although not usually one to soak in a tub when at home, now it seemed like the next big thing to heaven to so indulge.

"So, Claire, tomorrow we'll start bright and early. Okay?"

The fine hairs on the nape of Claire's neck tingled. Did Calder just use her first name? Did that mean they didn't have to go through all of the formal bullshit because Claire was nonmilitary?

Claire took a chance. "Captain Calder, do you prefer to be called Margaret? Or Maggie?"

Calder's eyes narrowed. "It's captain to you. Only friends call me Maggie."

Claire's cheeks flushed scarlet. Damn it. Strike two. "I'm sorry, Captain Calder. I didn't mean any disrespect. It's just that..."

Calder arched a brow.

Claire fidgeted. "I feel like we've gotten off on the wrong foot. I wanted to apologize for the other day. I didn't mean to offend you by criticizing your handwriting."

Dead silence hung between them. Claire held her breath. Here it comes. Calder was going to chew her up and spit her out before Claire could further prove herself.

"Let's get one thing straight, McCallum. I do not offend easily, and certainly not for something as stupid as a dig at my handwriting which is, in fact, chicken scratch."

Stunned, Claire asked, "You mean, you're not angry?"

Claire watched Calder run slim fingers through her tousled hair. The simple action sent shock waves of excitement coursing through her body.

"Hell, no. It'll take a lot more than that to piss me off. However, because of my scribble, you might want to do me a favor."

"Name it, Captain."

Calder handed Claire a notepad and pencil. "I'll dictate and you write. Okay?"

Claire nodded.

"I need a purchase order sent ASAP for the following: Ten boxes of crayons; twenty boxes of sidewalk chalk; fifty large drawing pads. A case of artist brushes and watercolor paints. And coloring books, lots of coloring books. Bubbles, yes, bubbles are a must."

Claire stopped writing. "Captain Calder?"

"Hmm?"

"This reads like a list of supplies for children rather than for troops."

"How quick you are on the uptake, recruit."

Claire's cheeks burned. "Care to elaborate?"

Calder winked and placed the tip of her index finger to her lips. "It's a secret."

As if on cue, Salvatore poked his head in her office. "I apologize for interrupting, Captain, but Langley's on the phone."

"This is where we part ways, Recruit McCallum. Can I count on you helping out tomorrow, say around noon?"

Claire nodded and stood. "Yes, Captain."

During her walk to ARC, Claire had time to evaluate her feelings. She knew her attraction to Calder was too soon and far too fast, but she was powerless over her emotions. She felt like a love-struck teenager or, worse, a dog in heat. And why was she getting all hot and bothered over a woman who may not be into women? Take a reality check, McCallum.

The more she thought about it, the more she believed that reality check could be damned.

Chapter Five

A fine, morning mist glistened on Claire's cheeks and matted her hair as she pedaled a bike to MSU.

She skidded to a stop in front of the main hangar, flipped down the bike's rusted kickstand, and dismounted. To her luck, she spotted Salvatore.

"Hi," Claire said in a cheerful tone.

"Hi, Chicken Scratch."

Claire winced, detesting the nickname. "Is Captain Calder in her office?"

"Nope. She's playing in the activity yard."

"Playing?"

Salvatore laughed. "Go see for yourself."

Claire rounded the corner of Medical Services and came to an abrupt halt. Ten yards from where she stood, Calder and two servicewomen were playing kickball with a group of Vietnamese children. There were twelve in all: eight boys and four girls. The girls wore simple cotton shifts and the boys, white T-shirts and cotton shorts. Their giggles and sounds of merriment brought an amused smile to Claire's lips.

Well, that explained the arts and crafts order. But what were children doing here? On a military base?

A sudden motion to the left caught Claire's attention. A Vietnamese girl stood beside a waist-high, wooden storage crate clutching a doll woven from straw. The child couldn't have been more than four or five years old. She had a faraway look in her eyes and the saddest expression Claire had ever seen in one so young.

Instinctively, Claire reached in her satchel for her camera. In one fluid movement, she popped off its lens cover, raised it to eye level, and zoomed in on the child's face.

At the sound of a rapid series of shutter clicks, the girl turned toward Claire with eyes wide with terror. She let out an ear-piercing shriek and took off running in the opposite direction.

"Shit," Claire said. "What the hell just happened?"

When Claire started to go after her, she heard someone shout her name. "Claire, don't."

Claire spun to see Calder rushing toward her.

"Captain Calder, I'm not sure what went wrong."

Calder eyed the camera and grimaced. "I know exactly what went wrong. It's your camera. The shutter clicks frightened her."

"How?"

"In the world she now lives in, many sounds are often foreign. Except maybe one, and that's the sound of a machine gun being engaged to fire."

"I'm not following you."

"The shutter clicks sound much like a weapon. I heard them too and, for a split second, I thought the base was under fire."

Claire gawked at her. "Oh, my God! You mean that little girl thought I was going to shoot her?"

"It may sound far-fetched to you, but if you'd gone through what Kimmy's gone through, hell, what all of these kids have gone through, you'd be running for cover, too."

"Kimmy?"

"Yes. Her full name is Kim Nguyen." Calder pronounced the first name as *Keem*.

Claire bit her lip and blinked back tears. "What happened to her? To them?"

"A firefight erupted in their small village. Details are sketchy. What we've gathered is the Viet Cong raided the village and killed all the adults. Our troops believe those VC bastards thought the villagers were U.S. sympathizers."

Hot bile burned Claire's throat. A memory flashed in her mind. A newscast of another massacre in a small Vietnamese village that happened years ago. She shuddered. "How awful. Why do you think the children were spared?"

"We later learned that they'd been on an outing in a paddy field. They were far enough away from the village for their presence to go undetected. Except for one."

Claire's stomach lurched. "Kimmy."

"Yes. When our troops were dispatched to investigate the cause of the firefight, they found poor Kimmy hiding beneath an old woman's dead body. They had to pry her tiny fingers loose from the woman's back. As TSN is the nearest base, they rounded up the others and brought them here. We've been taking care of them for weeks now, awaiting further orders."

"And no one in any of the villages is willing to adopt them?"

"In case you haven't noticed, there's a bloody shit storm going on. The villagers have enough problems protecting themselves and their children, let alone adopting others. It's a sad state of affairs right now, and I think the mentality is every man for himself, and that includes orphans."

Claire took a step toward where Kimmy had fled. "I have to find Kimmy and try to make her understand that I meant no harm."

Calder placed her hand on Claire's shoulder. "Not today. Let me have some time with her. It might help if you loaned me your camera, so I can show her it's not a weapon."

Disgusted with herself, Claire thrust the camera at Calder. "Take the damn thing. It's hasn't been of any use, anyway."

"Come on, Chicken Scratch, it's not as bad as all that. Besides, you'll have plenty of time to make it up to her."

"How?"

"You're going to be Kimmy's voice. Hell, you're going to be all of the orphans' voices so that you can help us to better understand and communicate with them. To teach us their way of life so that being here with us doesn't seem so frightening to them."

"I'll do whatever I can, especially for Kimmy."

"That's the spirit."

A deep voice sounded behind them. "Captain Calder?"

Claire turned and shaded her eyes with her hand to cut down on the glare.

"What's up, Salvatore?" Maggie asked.

"Your arts and crafts and medical supplies have arrived.

And a box of donated clothes and shoes for the children from the mainland."

Calder turned to Claire. "How are you at organizing?"

"I volunteered to stock shelves at the food bank back home every Sunday."

"Excellent." Calder eyed Claire's uniform. "Oh, and before I forget. There's a relaxed dress code here, so you can ditch the cute baby blues for jeans and a T-shirt if you want."

Claire blinked. Did Calder say cute? As in, Claire looked cute in her uniform? Or was she reading into every damn word she says? Enough. This was not the time to entertain romantic thoughts. Focus. There's serious work to be done.

Two hours later, Claire wiped sweat from her brow and broke down the last remaining cardboard box. Satisfied with her efforts, she looked up and sucked in air. Calder was bent over a carton of shoes, her firm, round ass within touching distance. Claire hadn't realized she was holding her breath until it came out in a whoosh. Calder turned before Claire could avert her eyes. Great. Now she thought Claire was a pervert.

"Looking at anything in particular, Recruit?"

Think, damn it. Think of an excuse. "Those little boy sneakers are adorable."

"Shoes, huh?"

"Yup. Shoes."

Calder wiped her hands on her pants and shrugged. "If you say so."

Red as a beet, Claire looked everywhere but into Calder's eyes. Calder checked her watch. "It's after five, Recruit. Time to call it a day."

At Calder's mention of the time, Claire burst into frantic motion.

"I said it's time to call it a day, Claire. Not flee from a fire."

"I need to be somewhere in less than a half hour."

"Somewhere?"

"At MARS, I mean, the Military Affiliate Radar Services station in sector three."

"I know what MARS means, goofball. Who are you phoning?"

"My parents. I'm sure they've received my letter by now."

"Good luck."

"Thanks. I think I'm going to need it."

****

Claire arrived at MARS with a few minutes to spare and took advantage of the extra time to calm her nerves and compose her thoughts. She'd scheduled her appointment for six, Eastern Standard Time, because her parents would be home, catching up on the evening news before supper. Her father would be sitting in his favorite easy chair with her mother perched on its arm, ready to pop into the kitchen when the oven timer sounded. The mental image caused an intense pang of homesickness to consume her. Tears filled her eyes and her breath hitched. She closed her eyes and waited for the emotional wave to pass. The last thing Mom and Dad need to hear was her breaking down.

Steeling herself, Claire poked her head into the MARS tent. As she didn't want to startle the officer manning the communication desk by barging in, Claire knocked on a wooden sign-in stand at the entrance.

The ham radio operator, a young serviceman with a close-cropped afro and warm brown eyes, looked up and smiled. "Hi, your name please?"

"Claire McCallum."

The operator checked her name off on a schedule sheet. "Come on in and take a seat. My name's Hatch. I'll be your operator during the call. Before we begin, let's review a few things you need to know from the get-go."

In an attempt to hide her nervousness, Claire sat on her hands so Hatch wouldn't notice them shaking. "Shoot," Claire said.

"You only have a few minutes to speak. Don't forget to say 'over' when you're finished your comment. That's how I and the other ham radio operator will know when to switch back and forth. Most importantly, do not tell the party you're speaking to where you are or what you're doing in Vietnam. Although this is a secure band, we can't take the risk of the opposition hacking into it. So, keep the conversation light, such as, the weather is beautiful, I hate the uniforms, meals taste like shit, blah de blah de blah. Stuff along that line. You'll only have a few minutes of air time. You'll know you're time is close to running out when I hold up my hands and finger count back from ten. Got it?"

"Got it."

"Groovy. Hold tight while I set the right frequency and secure a connection."

Claire waited what felt like an eternity for Hatch to finish and hand her a phone receiver.

"Whenever you're ready, Claire. My man on the other end's already informed your parents that you're on the line. They understand that only one person can talk at a time, and to try to keep the conversation short so everyone has a chance to speak."

For a few panic-stricken seconds, Claire couldn't find her voice. "Mom? Dad?"

Claire waited for her parents to respond. Hatch nudged her elbow. "Don't forget to say 'over.'"

"Oh, over."

"Claire!" her mother, Sherri, exclaimed. "Honey, it's so good to hear your voice. Over."

"That's ditto for me, too, Claire. Over," her dad, Mike McCallum, echoed.

Taken aback by their welcoming tones, Claire swallowed hard. "Mom? Dad? You're happy to hear from me? After what I did? Over."

"Well, sakes alive! What a silly question. Tell her, Mike. Over."

"We got your letter, and even though your mom and I hate to admit it, your reasons to return to Vietnam make sense. After all, it's your place of birth and where you spent your early years. We never thought that bringing you back with us to the states would leave you with unresolved feelings. We're sorry for that, honey. Over."

"It's just that I never had the chance to make peace, to truly say goodbye. Over."

"But why couldn't you have waited for peacetime to go? Over," Sherri asked.

"I needed to go back now, Mom. Over."

"Is it because of Minh? Over," Mike asked.

"In part. But not all the reason. Dad, there's so many orphans here. So many just like me. I want to make a difference. I want to help them to adjust. Over."

"But what about your safety? Over," Sherrie asked.

"Rest assured, I'm on a base that is far from any war zones. The ARC is taking good care of me. Over."

"How's the food?" her mother asked. "Are you eating right? No skipping meals? Over."

"The food's nothing to write home about, but I promise I'm eating three square meals a day. I've even made a few friends. One of them is a cap—" Claire stopped short. Hadn't Hack just warned her about not revealing any details? "Um, I mean, I feel as if I belong. So far, it's been a wonderful experience. Over."

"We're glad to hear it. Are you taking lots of photos? Over," Mike asked.

"Trying my best. Over."

"Oh good, because I've been clipping coupons for Fotomat from the Sunday paper for weeks now. If you mail me the film, I'll get them developed for you. Over."

"Groovy, Dad. Over."

"Most of all, Claire, your mother and I want to tell you how proud we are of you. Over."

Claire swiped at the tears dampening her cheeks. "That means so much to me, Dad. But enough about me. How are things at the office? And, Mom, are you still competing with Mrs. Winifred for head of the garden club? Over."

"Work is work. Same old, same old," Mike said. "I did finally hire a secretary. I couldn't keep up with the paperwork. Oh, hold on, Claire. Your mom wants to say something. Over."

Sherri's high-pitched voice pierced through the line. "In answer to your question, dear..." Her mother proceeded to drone on about how Winifred always got special attention, and that the voting process was rigged, and that Winifred was only part of the garden committee because her husband oversaw the arboretum.

Claire sighed, regretting asking the question in the first place.

Hatch held up his hands and began the countdown.

"Oh, Mom, sorry to cut you off, but there's a few seconds left. I want you and Dad to know how much I love you. And how much I miss you. Over."

"We know, Claire. We know. And we love you, too. Over."

Loud static crackled in her ear. Claire lowered the receiver and handed it back to Hatch so he could end the radio contact. Once signed off, Hatch placed a hand on her shoulder.

"Are you okay?"

Claire sniffed. "I got choked up for a moment. You don't know how much you miss people until you're separated from them."

"It'll get better. When are you scheduled for a home leave?"

"I haven't been here long enough to ask."

"Bummer."

Claire stood and extended her hand. Hatch took it in a firm grip.

"Same time next month?" she asked.

"You betcha."

****

Back at ARC, Claire popped into the mess hall for a bologna sandwich before heading to the sleeping tent. Although bologna wasn't her favorite deli meat, she hadn't had more than a handful of saltine crackers and a slice of white cheese all day and she was famished. If a stray shoe had been left around, Claire would've probably chewed its leather sole.

Although happy to have made contact with her parents, Claire also felt a pang of sadness. As she had come to learn so well, homesickness was something one never truly got over in a land so far away.

She spent the moments leading up to sleep going over

the day's events. Except for the unfortunate camera incident with Kimmy, the day had gone well. Calder had congratulated her on a job well done, which boosted her self-confidence and made her want to do more to please her, like leap tall buildings in a single bound, or do somersaults, or bend over backwards and touch her toes. As she drifted off to sleep, Claire wondered why pleasing Calder was so damn important to her. An inner voice whispered, "Because you like her. And it's not the type of like that is going to go away easily."

Chapter Six

Claire arrived at Medical Services at noon the following day, and headed straight toward the sound of squeals and giggles erupting from the activity tent. She peeked inside the tent's open flap and gasped at the sight of orphans running amok, smearing each other and service crew with colorful pastel paints. She burst into raucous laughter when she spotted Calder trying to fend off a boy who had lunged at her and splattered the front of her T-shirt with gobs of blue-green paint.

"Hey!" Claire shouted to Calder. "This looks like my kind of party. Care if I join in?"

Calder flashed her a grin. "Enter if you dare."

Claire didn't even have a chance to roll up her shirtsleeves when oomph, the wind was knocked out of her. She'd been attacked on her right by a girl wielding two paintbrushes saturated with red paint. Claire let out a scream and tried to defend herself, but her reflexes failed her. Another girl came at her from the left and shot a thin streak of yellow from an uncapped bottle down the front of her khakis.

"Hey!" Claire shouted. "No fair. That's two against one."

To her disbelief, yet another child snuck up behind her and palm-printed the back of her shirt. Defeated, Claire dropped to her knees and held up her hands. "Okay. I'm totally outnumbered. I surrender. I surrender."

With a triumphant cry, the trio of attackers rushed Claire and collapsed on top of her. Within seconds, more children joined in the growing human mound.

"Cherry on top! Cherry on top! Who wants to be the cherry?" Claire heard someone, maybe Calder, say.

"Me! Me!" a tiny voice cried. Claire let out a deflated whoosh of air when the cherry-topper added her weight to the pile.

"Okay, you little imps, I propose a truce!" Calder shouted. "Release the captive."

One by one, the weight on Claire's chest eased and she no longer felt entangled in a sea of flailing arms and legs.

Calder stood above her with her hand extended. "How are you faring, Chicken Scratch? I hope the little tykes didn't do any permanent damage."

Claire winced through a stabbing pain in her left rib. "Nothing I can't walk off."

Once on her feet, Claire took in the post-chaotic scene. The activity tent and its occupants resembled a tie-dye paint party gone berserk. "What the hell happened?"

"Not sure," Calder said, as she filled two paper cups with ice-cold water from a gallon jug. She handed Claire one before downing hers in a single gulp. Claire used every ounce of self-control not to reach out and wipe away the few droplets of water resting in the cleft of Calder's chin.

"One minute, all the kids were seated at picnic tables, dipping and dabbing their brushes in paint and creating colorful scenes on poster board. In the blink of an eye, they transformed into raging monsters."

"It looks like they had a ball."

"They did, and I'm glad. It gave them a chance to let off steam. Release pent-up anxiety. They've witnessed evils that no child should ever cast eyes on. Although I've tried my damnedest to learn the basics of the Vietnamese language, it's not enough to bridge the language barrier between them and us. It kills me that they're unable to fully express their pain. That's why I'm so glad you're here to not only help the children, but to help me to better understand them. Especially Kimmy. She's so much more traumatized than the others. What she's seen..."

Calder shuddered and her Claire's smile faded. "Yes, Kimmy. How is she? Were you able to show her the camera and explain that I never meant to frighten her?"

Calder's eyes lit up. For a brief moment, Claire caught a glimpse of an animated Calder, a happier Calder. "Yes! At first, she shied away from holding it, but with a little coercing, she came around. I demonstrated how to look through the lens and focus on an object before pressing the shutter button and then let her try. Once she got the hang of it, there was no stopping her. She's a regular little poser, that one. That is, until we ran out of film. Looks like I owe you a fresh roll."

A wave of relief flooded through Claire, making her feel weak at the knees. "You don't owe me anything. I'm forever in your debt."

Calder retrieved Claire's camera from a khaki duffel bag and handed it to her. "Consider your debt paid in full."

"Speaking of Kimmy… Where is she? I haven't seen her. But in the blitz attack, it's no wonder."

"Well, you may not have seen her, but you definitely felt her."

"I don't follow you."

"Do you remember the little kid who wanted to be the cherry on top?"

"You mean… No."

"Oh, yes. Our Kimmy leapt at the chance!"

Claire shook her head. "Why that little… I guess we're even."

Calder pointed to her far left where Kimmy, coated from head to toe in a purple haze, sat helping a female officer recap paint bottles. Claire's heart swelled with affection. Unlike the other day, Kimmy didn't look like a terrified little girl anymore. She looked like a regular kid, without a care in the world.

Calder shouted. "Hey, Kimmy! Say hello to Claire."

Kimmy looked up and grinned.

"See, no lasting effects," Calder said.

"Thank God."

"And she's eyeballing that satchel of yours up a storm. Not that I blame her, with all those colorful patches sewn on it."

Claire looked down at the khaki-green satchel. The patches were a kaleidoscope of embroidered colors with such expressions as 'Make Love, Not War,' 'Keep on Truckin',' and the *Laugh-In* classic line, 'Sock it to Me.' The remaining two patches were logos of two of her favorite bands, the Rolling Stones' protruding tongue, and the

Grateful Dead's dancing bears.

Claire skimmed her fingers across the satchel's rough fabric. "Oh, this? It's my dad's."

"Impressive."

"It was his way of bringing a little home-grown rock and roll and pop culture along in his travels when he worked with the ARC."

"It's a true depiction of the era."

"Yes. In wanting to keep up the tradition, I've collected a bunch of new ones, but haven't had the time to sew them on."

"That's a good thing."

"Why?"

Maggie nodded toward Kimmy. "I think you'll find Kimmy to be a willing helper."

"That's an excellent idea, Captain Margaret Anne Calder with an *e*."

Calder blinked in surprise.

"What?" Claire asked.

"Why did you address me in such a formal fashion?"

"A few days ago, you reprimanded me for calling you Maggie. You said only friends call you Maggie."

Calder's cheeks reddened. "Did I?"

"You did."

"Damn. How rude of me."

Calder thrust out her hand and Claire gripped it tight. "Please, call me Maggie. I insist on it, but only when we're not around anyone under my command. They'll get jealous."

Claire wanted to do an Irish jig and praise the heavens above. Instead, she asked, "Does that mean you now consider me a friend?"

Maggie's lips curled into a grin that rivaled the Cheshire Cat's. "Of sorts."

She eyed the tent and its paint-splattered children. "What do you say we round up these rug rats and herd them off to the showers? I hope they don't put up a fuss and I'm forced to use my hard-ass attitude on them. I hate when I have to do that."

Claire remembered her conversation with George.

"Speaking of being a hard-ass—" Claire bit her tongue, telling herself to zip it. But it was too late. Maggie was staring her down like a drill sergeant.

"What did you say?" Maggie asked.

"Nothing. It's nothing."

"It's definitely something, and it has to do with my ass. Go on. Spill the beans. I promise I won't bite."

"I heard that you can be quite..." Again, Claire hesitated.

Maggie arched a brow. "Difficult?"

Claire nodded.

Maggie snickered. "What can I say? Like father, like daughter."

"Your father served in the military?"

"Yes. Top brass."

"Is that why you joined? To follow in his footsteps?"

"Hell, no. I joined to spite him."

"I don't get it."

"Pop's the stereotypical male chauvinist pig. He believed that women tended the home and birthed children. Period. War was a man's arena. When I turned eighteen, I enlisted to prove him wrong."

"How did he react?"

"He cut off all ties with me. I haven't spoken to him in ten years."

Claire touched Maggie's shoulder. "I'm so sorry."

Maggie forced a smile. "It's okay. Like I said, it was a long time ago."

"So, is that why you remained in the military?" Claire asked. "To continue to spite your father?"

"Hell, no! I'm committed to the cause lock, stock, and barrel. It just took me a while to clear my head so I could accept my true calling of serving our country."

"The Air Force is lucky to have you."

"Some might disagree, which brings me back to my reputation on base. Truth be told, I've ruffled a few feathers while stationed at Tan Son Nhut."

"How so?"

"When I first arrived on base, I served as an assistant to Captain Moriarty, who oversaw the Medical Services division. Long story short, Moriarty detested having a female officer under his command. On more than one occasion, I overheard him bemoaning to his fellow officers that a 'woman's place should be in the home, either on her back for the nightly rumble in the jungle or preparing breakfast, lunch, and dinner."

Claire gawked at her. "He did not say that!"

"Oh, yes he did. Even though my credentials were second to none, he excluded me from meetings and denied me top logistical assignments. Right from the start, though, I knew he could be sloppy and that he'd eventually make a mistake. So, I waited. And I waited. And one day I discovered that his coordinates for a medical supply and ammo drop off in the field were completely off target."

"Meaning?"

"Meaning, that if that chopper had delivered its load using Moriarty's directive, the shipment would've landed in North Vietnamese or Viet Cong-occupied territory."

Claire's jaw dropped. "Christ, the enemy would've used our own ammo against us."

"Yes."

"So, what did you do?"

"I confronted Moriarty, but he laughed in my face and told me I didn't know shit. I had no choice but to go two ranks above him to reroute the mission."

"And they believed you?"

"She sure as hell did."

"She?"

"Lieutenant Colonel Agatha James reamed Moriarty a new asshole and demoted him to First Lieutenant. Shamed, the worthless sack of lard requested a transfer to another base."

"And who took his position?"

Maggie beamed "You're looking at her."

Claire clapped. "Bravo, Captain Calder. Bravo. So, you're a legend around TSN?"

"Yes, and the men hate it. They keep their distance, and that suits me fine."

"I met a fellow this morning who's also somewhat of a legend around base."

"Oh, yeah? Who?"

"His name's George, and he's a pit bull when it comes to playing ping-pong. He's friendly enough, although a little rough around the edges. He kind of reminds me of Popeye the Sailor."

Maggie picked at a splotch of paint on her shirt. "Oh, that's Waldron. Everyone on base knows Waldron. He's seen more war and bloodshed than most of us, thank God, will experience in our lifetime."

"He seems a weathered old soul."

"George may be weathered and old, but his memory's sharp as a tack. If you want to get a true history lesson, you better pick his brain fast. He's due to go home soon."

Maggie looked up. "Well, I'll be damned. It looks like our little angels got tired of waiting for us. They're already lined up at the showers."

****

A day's end, Claire left MSU and headed back to ARC's sector. Flutters of excitement coursed through her and she resisted the urge to skip past all things mundane. Today was a good day. No, it was a fantastic day. Claire finally felt she had a groove on with Maggie. Not only were they on a first-name basis, but they'd made a connection. She could feel it and, at this point Claire would take anything she could get.

Once showered, Claire kicked back on her lumpy cot and reviewed ARC's first aid manual until the persistent grumble in her stomach made her glance at her watch. Damn. No wonder she was starving. It was chow time.

As she headed to the mess hall, her thoughts again drifted to Maggie. Claire knew her crush on Calder was unrealistic. The woman was drop-dead gorgeous, self-assured, and well established in her career, whereas Claire still floundered. And grooving on a straight woman was fine in a fantasy world, but wouldn't hold much weight in the real world. Claire saw no harm in fantasizing about a life with Maggie, though. Age, career status, or experience didn't matter in her fantasy. And the sex—the thought of being intimate with Maggie made Claire moist between her thighs. Her stimulating daydream was interrupted by someone calling her name. She turned to see George hobbling toward her. "Are you stalking me, old man?" she teased.

George chortled and held up his arms. "Not my intention, little lady. As you seem to be going my way, I thought I'd walk with you."

"If your way is the mess hall, you're right on."

Claire slid her arm in his. I hear we're in for a treat. They're serving beef stroganoff tonight, which is one of my all-time favorites. I'm sure my mom's recipe would win, hands down, but beggars can't be choosers. I also promised her I'd take pictures of the food so that she wouldn't worry I'm not eating enough." Claire snapped her fingers. "I got it. You can be my food model."

"You want to photograph me holding a plate of noodles and meatballs?"

"At least I'm putting my photography skills to some use. It seems as if you can't take a damn picture around here without being told it's off limits."

"Most activities on base are top secret. If photographs, even innocently taken ones, happen to get in the enemy's hands, there'd be a cluster fuck. Pardon my French."

"So I've been told."

The beef stroganoff ended up being so tasty that both she and George went back for seconds.

"So, George, if you don't mind me asking. What brought you into military service?"

"Why my patriotic need to serve my country. What else?"

"I mean... You seem kind of old."

George grunted and swiped a napkin across his lips. "I'm what you'd call a career serviceman, which means I'm a repeat enlister."

Claire sucked a buttered noodle between pursed lips. "How many tours have you signed on for?"

George scratched his head. "Suffice it to say, I've spent many decades in the trenches. Military life is all I've known. It's all I've ever wanted to know. I serve as a liaison now, but that's soon to change. I'll be discharged soon."

"So you won't try to stay on?"

George stroked his stubbly chin. "If you hadn't noticed, I'm an old man with a limp, shit for eyesight, and the beginnings of what the doctors tell me is some type of debilitating arthritis. Not much left here for me to do."

"Is there anything you can do back home that involves the military?"

"Ah, yup. There is."

Claire leaned close. "Care to tell?"

"Me and my buds have decided to run our own VFW post."

"Your buds?"

"Sure! There's Dickey. He's the one whose ass I whooped the other night. Dickey's a decorated naval officer. He served in World War II, and he's a repeater, like me. And then there's Elwin and Leonard, who are the young'uns of the bunch. They're up for honorable discharge a few months after me."

"It sounds like your buds are a wonder team."

"I don't mean to brag, but we're the cream of the crop. The U.S. military's finest soldiers on and off the battlefield."

"I'm sure you'll succeed with your VFW plans."

"I hope so. I imagine it's not going to be easy trying to fit in with a society that often treats war veterans with zero respect."

"Maybe society will surprise you."

George cocked his head. "From your lips to God's ears, little lady." George conked the side of his head with a palm. "I just had a thought. I'm meeting up with Dickey and the boys tonight in the gaming tent. He's supposed to have my win money and a bottle of Jack. Want to come?"

"It depends. I need to translate some non-classified documents, but it shouldn't take me more than an hour. What time are you meeting?"

"Roughly in an hour."

"Then that should work out fine. Count me in."

"Great. Between the four of us, drinking booze and rehashing old war stories is what we do best."

****

To Claire's surprise, the gaming tent was deserted sans a girl and a guy huddled in a corner making goo-goo eyes at each other, and an elderly man seated at a high-top table.

"Definitely not the happening place tonight," Claire said.

George shrugged. "What did you expect? It's a week night. Oh, there's Dickey."

George grinned and clapped Dickey on the back. "Glad to see you brought the booze. Where's the other two?"

"Elwin and Leonard couldn't make it. Some lame ass excuse about having to get up early. I personally think they've got something going with a few of the Donut Dollies." Leonard looked at Claire. "Good evening, miss. Sorry to have to tell you that you're stuck with us old-timers tonight."

Claire slid onto a stool. "Old-timers are my favorite group of people." She extended her hand.

"Hi. I'm Claire McCallum. I'm an interpreter with the Red Cross."

Dickey gazed at her with the most piercing blue eyes she'd ever seen. "Hi, Claire, I'm Dickey."

"That's Chief Naval Officer Richard Pearson," George said.

"No formalities amongst friends, George," Dickey said.

"Dickey served on the U.S.S. Indianapolis when the opposition torpedoed it in forty-five."

Claire gasped. "Oh, my God!"

Dickey frowned. "George likes to bring up ghosts from the past, whereas I would rather leave them to rest."

"But you were a hero, Dickey," George exclaimed. "For cripe's sake, you were part of the Navy's top-secret mission to deliver nuclear parts to be used in the Little Boy bomb."

"That's what the history books are for, George."

George wouldn't let it rest. "Dickey and close to a thousand men were left stranded in the ocean. Between exposure, dehydration, and those fucking shark attacks, it's a wonder he made it out of the water alive."

Dickey grimaced. "I was fortunate. Let sleeping dogs lie, Waldron."

George must've finally got the hint. He reached for the bottle of Jack and cracked the seal. "Let's toast."

Dickey snagged three shot glasses from a side bar and lined them up for George's pour.

In unison, they reached for their glasses and raised them high.

"What do we drink to?" Claire asked.

"To wars won and lives lost but never forgotten," Dickey said.

"Hear. Hear."

****

An hour later, Dickey rose unsteadily. "Time to call it quits for the night, fellow comrades," he said. "Early bugle call and all."

George guffawed. "You mean early morning grub call. You haven't stood at attention in years. Admit it, Pearson. You're a lightweight when it comes to holding your liquor."

"And you're a legend in your own mind. How's anyone able to get a word in edgewise with you jabbering all night long?"

George muttered something under his breath and poured another shot.

Dickey reached for Claire's hand. "It's been a pleasure. I hope we can do this another time. Maybe when I win the next ping-pong tournament and George has to ante up."

"Dream on, pansy," George said.

Claire smiled. "I look forward to it."

Once Dickey left, Claire said. "I like your buddy. He's a man of few words."

"Dickey's a man scarred, but he puts up a tough front. He's a strong old bird."

"I think you're pretty strong, too, George."

"Nah. Made my share of mistakes in this lifetime. You can be sure of that."

Claire waited for him to continue. When he didn't, she said, "Well, don't leave me hanging old man. What's your worst mistake?"

George's lips compressed into a thin white line. "I don't

want to talk about it."

"I'm sorry, George. I didn't mean to hit a sore spot."

"No harm done, little miss." George capped the bottle of Jack. "We best be off. It's getting late. You don't want Buns breathing fire up your ass."

They walked in silence, with only a nod from George when they parted ways.

Claire felt like crap. She shouldn't have been so damn nosy. Damn alcohol. The last thing she'd wanted to do was hurt George's feelings.

When she finally settled in, Claire dreamt of death.

Chapter Seven

At dawn, Claire awoke to a pounding headache. Her mouth felt as if she'd swallowed a bale of cotton. She popped two aspirin, washed them down with gulps from the water fountain, and headed off to the showers. She turned on the overhead faucet and grimaced. Damn. The water was lukewarm at best. Well, at least the pressure was steady and she wouldn't feel as if she were wearing a layer of soap scum all day. As she lathered up, she wondered what today would be like. Would she be a welcoming presence or a hindrance? Claire inwardly chastised herself. Why was she so damn hard on herself? And, did it matter if Maggie liked her? She was here for the children. To make their lives better. Period.

Claire's heart swelled like a balloon when Maggie met her at the entrance of MSU with a smile and a steaming mug of coffee.

"You look a little gray around the gills there, Chicken Scratch."

Claire rubbed the side of her temple and winced. "I'm working through a hangover from last night."

"Hangover, huh? I didn't take you for the party animal type."

"I'm not. Thus, the headache."

Maggie smirked. "May I ask who you had the pleasure of drinking with?"

"George and his buddy, Dickey."

Maggie chortled. "Hell, girl, I told you to listen to their war stories, not match them shot for shot. Those old-timers sure know how to hold their liquor."

"So I found out. What are you up to today?"

"Working on the kids' nutrition menu for this week, which is turning out to be a damn frustrating task. Stock rations are slim this month. So, I've had to resort to cutting the menu down to bare bones items like corn flakes, bread, powdered milk, cheese, and a lot of canned vegetables. Oh, and PB and J."

"I love PB and J! It's my all-time favorite, hands down," Claire said.

Maggie smiled. "Ah, so you have a sweet tooth?"

"Oh, yes! When my adoptive parents introduced me to it, I went crazy. I had to have it for breakfast, lunch, and dinner. It's even better on crackers."

"Well, I guess this menu will have to do. It's a shame we can't borrow one of the villagers to cook for us. As it is, they've got their hands full feeding their own."

"You know, I may be able to help you out in that area."

Maggie blinked. "Really? You can type, interpret, and cook, too?"

Claire shrugged. "I can manage."

"Well, hot damn. I don't have an ARC recruit working for me. I have a Wonder Woman, missing the sexy outfit. I would love for you to put your cooking talents to work. There's a kitchen in the Officers' Building. We could use that. And—"

"Captain Calder!"

They turned to see Salvatore rushing over.

Maggie grimaced. "Well, this can't be good."

Salvatore stood at attention and saluted Maggie. "Something's happened, Captain. Red alert."

Maggie tensed. "Get the others. We'll meet in the map room."

Maggie turned to Claire. "I'm sorry I have to cut our afternoon short."

"Understood. I'm sure I can be of use somewhere."

Maggie squeezed Claire's arm and strode off.

Claire spotted Kimmy sitting off by herself, cradling her handmade doll, while the other orphans shaped forms out of colored wads of modeling clay. Claire frowned. Why wasn't she participating with them?

Kimmy grinned when she saw her, revealing a few missing teeth. She dropped her doll and ran toward Claire. Meeting her halfway, Claire dropped to one knee to wrap her tiny form in a warm hug. When she released her, Claire pointed toward the other children.

"Why aren't you playing with the others?" Claire asked

in Vietnamese.

"I didn't want to miss seeing you."

"Me? You chose to watch out for me instead of have fun?"

Kimmy smiled and reverted to English. "Claire is fun."

Well, how about that. "Okay, I get it. Sculpting mustn't be your thing. How about trying something new?"

"Da!"

Claire reached for Kimmy's hand and led her to an empty picnic table. Once seated, Claire placed her satchel on the wooden tabletop. She reached inside and slid out the embroidered patches she'd purchased stateside, a spool of black thread, and a stitching needle she'd borrowed from Laundry Services. Kimmy watched Claire with wide-eyed fascination.

"Kimmy, we're going to sew all these cool patches on this satchel. I want you to help me make it beautiful, so I want you to hold the fabric tight while I sew. Can you do that for me?"

Kimmy nodded.

"Great." Claire positioned Kimmy's fingers on the fabric and spread them across it. She gave Kimmy's shoulders an encouraging squeeze. "Perfect."

Within an hour, a new set of pop culture patches were sewn into place. Claire beamed as Kimmy traced the ridged embroidery with her fingertips.

Claire pointed at a patch of a lime-green flower with a yellow smiley face in its center. "*Khá*," Claire said, using the Vietnamese word for pretty. "*Khá* means pretty."

Kimmy looked into Claire's eyes. "Pretty."

Claire clapped her hands. "Yes. Pretty."

She proceeded to point at other patches with Kimmy repeating the word each time. When Claire felt certain Kimmy understood the word's meaning, she cupped Kimmy's chin in her hands. "You, my dear Kimmy, are very pretty."

Kimmy giggled and mimicked Claire's gesture by grabbing Claire's cheeks. "Pretty. Claire is very pretty, too."

"Aw, kid. Now you made me blush."

"Can I show the others what we made?" Kimmy asked.

Claire handed Kimmy the satchel. "Be my guest."

****

Claire spent the remainder of the afternoon working on the orphans' class schedule. She estimated an hour for each of the major subjects, including Math, English, Reading, and Writing. That left the children with their afternoons free to do as they pleased.

She'd retrieved her satchel from Kimmy and walked to MSU. Before she could mount her bike, Claire saw Salvatore hotfooting it toward her.

"Claire. I'm glad you're still here. Captain Calder would like to see you."

Claire found Maggie seated at her desk rifling through a stack of papers. She knocked and waited for Maggie to look up. When she did, Claire gasped. Maggie's eyes were red-rimmed and swollen, and her complexion ashen. Claire's stomach wrenched. *She's been crying.*

"My God, Maggie, what's happened?"

"The worst thing that can happen."

"Red alert?"

Maggie rubbed her eyes and pushed back from the desk. "Yes. I've spent the entire afternoon coordinating search and recovery efforts."

"Search and recovery?"

"Body retrieval."

"Bo—"

Maggie's walkie-talkie sounded. She snatched it off the desk and depressed the talk button. "Calder here. Over."

"Debriefing's about to start, Captain."

"I'll be right there. Over."

Maggie stood and gathered the papers into a folder. She looked at Claire. "How are you at taking notes?"

"Even better than my typing skills."

"Come along, then."

****

A handful of elderly men, with an adornment of medals

and stripes on their uniforms, sat around a large, oblong table. All sported stern expressions. So as not to seem intrusive, Claire sat in a chair in a far corner of the room, directly opposite from Maggie. Sal set next to her. When their eyes met, they exchanged nods.

One of the officers cleared his throat.

"Captain Calder. Do you have a final count of the casualties?"

"Fifty confirmed dead, Sir."

The officer slammed an open palm on the table. "That's half a unit for Christ's sake. Any survivors?"

"Ten, Sir. They were choppered out to a medship, Sir."

"And the rest?"

Maggie bit her lower lip. "Upwards of thirty soldiers left on the battlefield, Sir."

Claire clamped a hand across her mouth to keep from crying out.

"Recovery efforts?" another officer asked.

"Ongoing. The North Vietnamese are still very active in the area, Sir."

"Site maps?"

Sal stood and rolled out a large map of the besieged area. The officers stood and hovered over the map as Sal pointed out coordinates.

Aghast at what she'd heard, Claire gripped the pen tighter and tried to keep up with the verbal exchange. Oh, God. Oh, God. Oh, God. Soldiers left to die? She couldn't have heard that right.

Minutes later, the meeting adjourned and only Claire and Maggie remained in the conference room.

Maggie stood and rounded the table to sit beside her.

"I'm sorry, Claire. I hadn't intended to introduce you to the tragedies of war so soon. The last thing I wanted to do was blindside you."

Claire fought back tears. "Maggie, you said soldiers were left to die."

Maggie grimaced. "Claire, let me explain. The NC launched four separate missile attacks in an area not much bigger than a couple of football fields. For most soldiers on the ground, death was instantaneous. For others…"

"You mean the injured, right? That means they survived the initial attack. Why weren't they flown out with the others? Why weren't they given medical treatment?"

Maggie let out a haggard breath. "They were too far gone, Claire. Their injuries were so severe that they didn't have a chance of surviving."

Claire recoiled as if she'd been physically slapped. "How do you know that? Who makes such a call whether a soldier lives or dies?"

"We have trained medics on the ground who are left with the hard decision of whether a soldier's life is past saving."

Claire's voice rose in pitch. "So, they essentially play God? No one gets to play God, Maggie."

"Claire, I know this may sound cold-hearted, but to transport every fatally injured soldier from the line of fire to a medical treatment facility is dangerous. Choppers are only on the ground minutes, and can only transport a limited amount of injured at a time. And the injured who are transported are the ones with the best chance of survival."

"So the worst are left to die?"

"The ones beyond saving? Yes."

Claire's insides turned to jelly. "This war is a fucking nightmare," she whispered.

"Yes, and one none of us can seem to wake up from."

Claire shuddered.

Maggie whispered. "Are you going to be okay?"

"Shit, no. Until this goddamn war is over, I'm never going to be okay."

Silence rained heavy as both Claire and Maggie grappled with their emotions. After a time, Maggie spoke. "Claire, it's late. You should go back to ARC. You've had some heavy shit laid on you, and I think it'd be wise for you to take some time to clear your head."

"But I want to help."

Maggie smiled. "Of course you do but, for now, give yourself a rest."

Claire rubbed her eyes. "I'm sorry I got so emotional. I know that everything is being done to save lives in the field. It's just so hard for me to accept death as a final option even when it's a cold, hard fact for some. In a perfect world, I want the fighting to stop, and no other lives destroyed."

"Yes, if we only lived in a perfect world. Seriously, Claire. I want you to rest up. That's an order. Tomorrow is another day."

****

Back at ARC, Claire forced herself to eat a BLT sandwich despite the bacon being undercooked, the mayonnaise watery, and the lettuce wilting. Each bite made her want to vomit, but she swallowed past her disgust. She couldn't stop thinking about the bloody, mutilated bodies of American soldiers being left to die where they lay. It was barbaric.

The sound of dishes clattering roused her from her morbid thoughts. When she realized she was the last diner in the mess hall, she gathered her belongings and made a quick exit.

A voice shouted. "Hey, Claire! Wait up!"

Claire turned to see Quincy.

"Don't get too close," Quincy said. "I'm sweating like a pig, and I'm sure I smell like one, too. Off to the showers for me."

"Where are you coming from?" Claire asked.

"Dance practice. How about you?"

"Mess Hall. Late dinner."

"I caught up with you to tell you that you got a package today. I put it on your cot. I think it's from your folks."

"Thanks, Quincy."

Quincy peered at her. "Hey, are you okay? You look like shit."

"Rough day."

"Want to talk about it?"

Claire shook her head.

"Okay. I dig it."

****

Upon entering the sleeping tent, Claire collapsed onto her cot and reached for the envelope. She glanced at the return address: McCallum, Hobarth, NY. She hefted the envelope's weight from one hand to the other. Heavy.

Curious, Claire ripped open the seal and upended its contents. A carefully folded letter and a stack of flavored candy bars plopped onto the mattress.

"Priorities first," Claire said, as she ripped open the candy wrapper and took a hefty bite of a chocolate-flavored taffy before reaching for the letter.

Dearest Claire,

As always, you're in our thoughts and in our prayers. I thought giving you the lowdown on what's happening in Hobarth might make you feel closer to life back home. Let's start with Nosy Nellie Farrow. My, she started a rumor that could curl the one hair left on a bald man's head...

Claire smirked in spite of her depressed mood. Typical mom. Just as much a busy body as the rest of the town. The letter went on to recount neighbor feuds, church bake-offs, and general town gossip, all of which Claire couldn't give a damn about. Except for Father Joseph's Sunday sermon on praying for the war to end and the troops abroad to return home. That, indeed, was a prayer worth praying.

Claire teared up and swiped at her eyes with the back of her hand. Her vision again blurred when she read her father's note beneath her mother's signature.

We hope you're making lifelong friends. Talk soon.

Much love, Dad.

Sniffling, Claire slid open her dresser drawer and placed the goodies from home next to her satchel for safe keeping.

Lifelong friends, huh? Would Maggie be a part of her life after the war ends? What would Mom and Dad think of her? Would they be as charmed by her as Claire was?

An overhead speaker blast interrupted her musings.

"Phone call for Recruit McCallum. Phone call."

Claire bolted forward. A phone call? For me?

Claire stood and padded to a wall-mounted phone beneath a lit exit sign.

"Hello?"

"Claire?"

"Yes?"

"It's Captain Calder. I mean, Maggie."

Maggie. Excitement swirled within her, like riding a turbulent wave to shore.

"Maggie. How did you...?"

"Base directory, silly. Look, I couldn't stop thinking about you and what happened today. It's a hard pill to swallow, especially when you're new to all this."

"Experiencing the horrors of war was inevitable. I knew volunteering in Vietnam wasn't going to be a pleasure walk. I knew what I was going to be up against."

"Still."

A few beats of silence. "Maggie?"

"Yes?"

Claire hesitated. Did she dare ask? Damn yes, she did. "You were worried about me?"

"Of course I was worried about you. You're someone very..."

"Very?" Claire prodded.

"Special. You're a very special person, Claire. And far be it for me to cause you any undue upset."

Claire smiled. "Thank you for caring. It means a lot."

"Good. So, what do you say to my giving you a tour of the base?"

"I kind of got the tour the first day I arrived. From what I recall, the scenery's drab, upon drab, upon drab."

Maggie laughed. "There's more to see beyond TSN than its military presence, Claire. Besides, I thought it might help us to forget about the endless bloodshed, if only for a little while."

"But I thought we were banned from roaming the countryside."

"What I have to show you is still on base, if off the beaten track. I promise you won't be disappointed and that you won't get into any trouble."

"When?"

"Tomorrow."

Claire grinned like a child given sweets. "That sounds wonderful."

"Glad to hear it. I'll pick you up bright and early. Good night."

"Good night."

As soon as Claire hung up the phone she slapped both her cheeks until they stung. Was she dreaming, or did Maggie Calder call to say she was thinking about her? And that she wanted to spend time with her?

Wow. If ever there was a silver lining at the end of a shitty day, it was that phone call.

Chapter Eight

For once, Claire wasn't awoken by blaring bugles, shrill whistles, or screeching tires. She felt well rested and chalked that up to exhaustion and a dreamless sleep. And then there was Maggie's phone call and the promise of spending an entire day with her in a non-military fashion. Her heart swelled with excitement. She couldn't wait. Assuming sight-seeing meant some form of physical exertion, she pulled her hair into a ponytail, and opted for dungarees and peds. She grimaced when she noticed the tread on her sneakers was wearing thin. She made a mental note to have her mom send a new pair.

Claire exited the tent right as Maggie pulled up, riding a motorbike.

Claire eyed it skeptically. "You know, I've heard those things are dangerous."

Maggie smiled. "Depends on who's driving it."

"How do I know I can trust you?" she teased.

Maggie threw back her head and laughed. "You don't. But hop on anyway."

Once Claire mounted, Maggie reached behind for her hands. "Slide up against me, Claire, and hold tight around my waist. Some areas are going to be bumpy, and I don't want you bouncing off the back and landing in the dirt."

The heat radiating from Maggie's back had Claire's nipples standing at attention. Oh, Lord. She desperately hoped Maggie couldn't feel her tits poking her in the back. In this heat, Claire sure as hell couldn't tell her she was cold.

Exhilaration swelled within her, making her want to scream so loud she'd wake the dead. Instead, she took in the sights as Maggie steered the motorbike past everything military. Soon, the cement and paved roads used by service personnel faded away and were replaced with narrow, dirt paths. Maggie veered to the left at a fork in the road and urged the bike on until the lush foliage became too dense for the bike to maneuver.

Maggie cut the engine. "Here's where we get off. The terrain's a bit rough so we need to go on foot from here on out. I'll forewarn you, though, that it's a steep climb."

She held the bike steady so Claire could dismount first. Goosebumps rose along the nape of Claire's neck and fore-arms. Damn. Another dead give-away of how Maggie made her feel.

Maggie adjusted her satchel. "I'll lead and you follow close behind. And watch out for palm and bamboo plants."

"Oh, you don't have to warn me about them. Their fronds and shoots are as sharp as knives and can leave a nasty scar on your skin. I have more than one to prove it."

Like an overeager, adoring puppy, Claire followed behind Maggie. They hadn't gone far when Claire tripped on an overgrown tree root and stumbled hard against Mag-gie's back. Maggie laughed. "Hey, Chicken Scratch. I said keep close, not on top of me."

"Sorry."

For the next ten minutes the terrain rose ever higher in elevation, forcing Claire to use muscles she hadn't flexed in ages. Sweat poured down her face and stung her eyes.

"You weren't kidding about the steep climb, were you?" Claire panted.

"Hang in there, Claire."

When Maggie reached behind and gripped Claire's hand, Claire felt a tingly sensation thrum through her like a low, electric current.

Five yards farther, Maggie stopped short. "What I want to show you is just past that fruit grove. Would you humor me and close your eyes? I truly want this to be special for you."

Claire gulped. "Sure."

Ten steps later, Maggie said. "Okay, on the count of three, you can open your eyes. One. Two. Three."

Claire was adrift in a dream. Either that or she'd died and gone to heaven. The mountain top overlooked not only the entire base, but offered a faraway glimpse of a teal-col-ored ocean and a series of purpled-hued mountains flanking the expanse on two sides. A brilliant sun glistened across the water, making it sparkle like tiny shards of glass.

"Exquisite, isn't it?" Maggie whispered.

"Yes."

Maggie pulled out a pair of binoculars from a side satchel. "Here. These are high mag."

Claire raised the dual lenses and adjusted focus. "Wow. You aren't kidding. Is that the South China Sea?"

"Yes."

"It's a wonder. As a child, I often fantasized about constructing my own raft out of split bamboo and wood and sailing it, exploring the world.

"An adventurer at heart, huh?" Maggie teased.

Claire nodded. "An adventurer with an extremely vivid imagination. I can't tell you how happy I am to see it again, even if from afar. It brings back so many memories. And then there's the smells."

"Smells?"

"The flowers, silly. The intermingling scents of marigolds and orchids, of peach blossoms and yellow blossoms. It's intoxicating. This is a perfect little oasis."

"That's the way I felt the first time I stumbled on this spot. You can't imagine how many times I've envisioned sneaking away to lie on the sand and watch the waves lap at the shoreline. Or gaze upon the steady ebb and flow of the tide. But this is as far as I can get, at least for now, and I'm okay with that. Up here, I feel far removed from the goings on below. I can be an observer, not a participant."

"It's glorious!"

Maggie plopped down on the grass and motioned for Claire to join her. "Is this not the best day since your arrival at Tan Son Nhut?"

"Hands down."

"I so wanted to share this with you. Give you a sense that Vietnam, the Vietnam you knew as a child, still exists. That not all places are battle-ravaged. And, I thought you could use a friend of the same persuasion to show you the ropes."

Claire sputtered. Was that Maggie's none-too-subtle way of letting her know that she knew Claire was gay?

"Persuasion?" Claire asked. "What do you mean by a

certain persuasion?"

Maggie looked her dead in the eyes. "You know exactly what I mean. And, no need to get all flustered. Being of the same persuasion, my instincts are honed to perfection, not to mention I caught you staring at my ass on more than one occasion."

Busted. Wait, did Maggie intentionally out herself? "I don't know—"

Maggie chuckled. "There's no need to explain. That's not why I brought you here. I feel very comfortable with you, and sharing my secret makes me feel freer to talk about things the down-below crew consider taboo. I hope you feel the same way."

Claire drew her knees up to her chin and gazed seaward. "I do."

"However, since we're on the subject... Was it hard for you? Coming out?"

Claire plucked a blade of grass and sucked on its root. "Not really. It was a gradual process. I mean, besides being the stereotypical tomboy, I knew from a very young age that I wanted to impress girls with my wit and charm more than boys."

"Me, too. I knew it for sure the first time I kissed a girl."

Claire leaned back on her elbows. "How old were you?"

"I think ten."

"Cradle robber!" Claire chided.

Maggie scowled. "Cradle robber, my ass. The girl was two years older than me and it's not like we ripped each other's clothes off and did the down and dirty. It was a kiss prompted by a dare. A very sweet, very soft kiss. How about you?"

"Crushes all through high school and then, a heavy make-out session in college with a drunk classmate."

"And since then?"

"Hits and misses. Nothing serious."

"So, no broken heart?"

Claire shook her head. "How about you? Any lost loves?"

"Just one."

From Maggie's curt response, Claire didn't pry further.

"So, Claire, now that you're on a military base run primarily by men, I think it wise to advise you that you shouldn't flaunt your gayness. It's not accepted here. Hell, some of these bastards would have you tarred and feathered if they knew, and the top brass would turn a blind eye. Believe me, I've seen it happen."

"I totally get it. I know the boundaries." Claire grimaced and sat up. "It's just so damn frustrating. You'd think that there would be worse things to worry about in wartime than two women or two men digging each other."

Maggie held up her hands and made the quote sign with her fingers. "It's because we aren't the norm."

Claire snickered. "As if there is a norm."

Maggie stretched out her legs and flexed her ankles. "So, we have our own little secret to share. I think that's kind of cool."

"It's totally cool."

"And maybe, one day, you'll find love for the first time, and me the second time around. The challenge will be in finding the right one, for both of us."

"No easy task," Claire said.

"Stranger things have happened."

****

Once back in MSU with time to spare before lunch, Claire held the motorbike steady so Claire could dismount first. Claire rubbed her sweaty palms on her jeans. "Thanks for showing me your secret spot."

Maggie winked. "Stick with me, kid, and I'll show you the world."

"The world, huh?"

"Well, maybe just snippets, for now. That's what lifetimes are for, right?"

Great balls of fire. Was she mistaken, or was she crazily alluding to a future together?

Before Claire could comment, a child shouted. "Maggie! Claire!"

They turned to see Kimmy running toward them, clutching

a small stack of colored paper. By the time Kimmy reached them, she was sweaty and panting like she'd run a marathon. "Hey, little girl," Claire said, bending over to stroke her silky black hair. "Take a breath before you pass out. What's all the fuss about?"

"Will you make origami shapes with me?"

Claire grinned and motioned toward a wooden picnic table. "Sure. The concept's new to me, but how can I refuse?"

Seated side by side, Claire watched Kimmy fold the paper into sections then angles that, in the end, turned out to form the shape of a yellow butterfly.

"Now that is what I call super groovy, Kimmy. Can I try?"

Kimmy let out a whoop and thrust a green sheet of paper into Claire's hands. Claire fumbled with the paper, trying to mimic Kimmy's actions. After a minute of folding, unfolding, and folding again, Kimmy laughed.

"Claire, you are so silly. Let me help you."

Claire threw up her hands and rolled her eyes at Maggie. "By all means, kiddo."

Within an hour, and with Kimmy's help, Claire created a red crab, a green turtle, and three multicolored songbirds.

"These are fantastic, Kimmy," Claire said. "So fantastic that I have an idea. Why don't we string all of these shapes together and I'll hang them over your bed, so you can gaze up at them every night? Would you like that?"

"Yay!" Kimmy shouted and flung herself into Claire's arms. Surprised by the sudden gesture, Claire felt her body at first stiffen, then loosen as she returned the hug.

Maggie, who had watched Claire and Kimmy interact in silence, glanced at her watch.

"I hate to break up this little paper party, but if we don't hurry, we might miss lunch. Remember, it's tomato soup day."

Claire stood and reached for Kimmy's hand. "You heard the boss lady, Kimmy. Up and at 'em."

As they strolled toward the mess tent, Maggie and Claire hung back to talk.

"That was incredible," Claire said. "Kimmy was so

open. So...”

“Trusting?”

“Yes. She trusted me. Hey, why didn’t you join in?”

“I didn’t want to take away from your moment. And, I must say, you shined.”

Claire lowered her head so Maggie couldn’t see her burning cheeks. “Yep. I sure as hell did.”

“Whether you realize it or not, Claire, that little girl is forming a tight bond with you. Hell, ever since you jumped into the paint fight the other day and let the kids tackle you, they flock to you like moths to a flame.”

“What can I say? I’m a big kid at heart.”

“Well, it’s obvious Kimmy, in particular, is crazy about you.”

“The feeling’s mutual. I love hanging around with her. It’s like she’s my little shadow.”

“Indeed. You look very much like mother and daughter.”

A few beats of silence passed. “Maggie?”

“Hmm?”

“What’s going to happen to them once the war’s over?”

“No formal decision’s been made. I imagine some will be flown to safe havens in bordering countries.”

“You mean refugee camps, right?”

Maggie’s tensed. “Afraid so.”

“That sounds horrible.”

“As sad as it is, it’s reality.”

The idea formed seconds before Claire voiced it. “Would it sound crazy if I told you that after the war’s over, I’d like to adopt Kimmy?”

A few beats of silence passed before Maggie responded. “Considering you haven’t known her all that long? Yes.”

Claire suddenly felt foolish. “Yes, of course you’re right. Never mind me. I’m just thinking aloud.”

“Your heart’s in the right place. That’s as good a start as any.” Maggie stopped short. “I’ve been meaning to ask. Before all hell broke loose the other day, you mentioned something about cooking.”

“I did.”

“Were you serious?”

"As serious as a heart attack."

"Does tomorrow work for you?"

"Uh… Sure."

"Great. How about I have Sergeant Salvatore escort you into the neighboring village this afternoon so you can barter for whatever you need. Apparently, you're not the only Vietnamese woman with a sweet tooth."

"That would be groovy!"

"Consider it done."

****

Although TSN's east gate stood within shouting distance, the chance to escape its confines and walk on fresh soil, surrounded by thick underbrush and tropical plants, invigorated Claire. Not only was she excited to interact with her own people, but Maggie had given her the go ahead to take as many pictures as she wanted. She snapped a photo of a woman's age-spotted, weathered hands covered with flour, kneading a doughy mixture. Another shot homed in on a woman weaving strips of bamboo into a bowl-like creation. Claire felt like a kid let loose in a candy shop. Twice she had to swap out film.

One half hour into the field trip, Salvatore said. "I know that for you, this is a blast to the past, but it's getting late. We need to get back."

Claire frowned. "Okay. Just one more shot and we can leave, Sergeant."

"Please, call me Sal."

Claire startled Sal by taking a close-up photo of him, before she reached into her satchel and pulled out a jar of peanut butter and a jar of grape jelly. She held them out to three Vietnamese women and spoke a few sentences in Vietnamese. Moments later, Claire and Salvatore walked away with a satchel filled with fresh produce and chopped chicken chunks. When Claire glanced back to wave at the women, she burst out laughing. The women had already opened the jelly jar and were taking turns dipping their pinky fingers in for taste tests.

Chapter Nine

At daybreak, Claire hustled to the Officers' Building. She looked up at the two-story brick structure and whistled. "It must be nice to be an officer and not have to sleep in tents."

She opened the glass door and walked to the end of a long corridor before turning right into an open kitchen area.

She smiled. Sal had gone out of his way to line up the acquired fresh veggies, herbs, and ingredients for a marinade on a long wooden table, and had placed a mound of dried rice noodles in a wooden bowl. Claire glanced at a scribbled note taped to the refrigerator.

Chicken's chilling. Don't forget to save me some. Sal.

A giggle from behind made her turn. Hmm. No one there. Another giggle, higher in pitch. Claire played dumb. "My. My. I must be hearing things, or there's a bunch of elves playing tricks on me. I wonder which one it could be?" she asked in Vietnamese.

Claire turned away from the giggles and whispers coming from behind a curtained storage area and hummed an upbeat tune. Swoosh, then the pitter patter of little feet. Claire silently counted to ten, giving the intruders ample time to reveal themselves, before spinning on them with arms raised and a monstrous sneer on her face.

"Hah! Caught you, my little mischief makers!"

Kimmy and two other orphans, one male and one female, shrieked in surprise and then delight. Claire crouched and enfolded all three children in a hug that ended up turning into a tickling match.

"Okay. Okay. I give. I give. Get off me, you bunch of rug rats." Once she'd caught her breath, Claire asked. "What are you doing up with the sun?"

"We came to help you cook," Kimmy said.

Claire eyed the trio. "All three of you?"

The trio nodded in unison.

"Well then, let's get to it." Claire motioned toward the long table. "Sit, please."

Claire filled three large metal mixing bowls with tap water and placed them on the table with a hand towel beside each. She spoke in Vietnamese so there'd be no question of her being misunderstood. "First things first. I need one of you to wash some lettuce, another bean sprouts, and another cilantro and mint. When rinsed, you can lay them on the towels to dry."

As the children set to their tasks, Claire focused on preparing the marinade.

Another set of footsteps entered the room. Claire chuckled at the sight of Maggie holding a floral-patterned apron.

"Cute apron. It reminds me of something my mother would wear."

"Why are the children here?"

"Helping out."

Maggie grimaced when she saw a girl flick a handful of water into a boy's face.

"They look like they're making more of a mess than helping out."

Claire shrugged. "Every little bit helps. This is a team effort, and that includes you, Captain Calder."

Maggie sniffed the air. "Ah, is that what I think it is?"

"It's nuoc cham. Fish sauce marinade."

Maggie's eyes lit up. "That's right. Me and my damn linguistic handicap for not remembering the name. The aroma is unmistakable. And, might I ask, what you are serving the sauce with?"

"Chicken, which is where I might need your help. How are you at grilling?"

"I can handle basic BBQ, Claire."

"Good. There's a bowl of raw chicken in the fridge that needs tending to."

"Besides the sauce, what are you making?"

"Bun Ga Nuong."

"Huh?"

"Lemongrass chicken with diced up carrots, cucumbers,

and onions over pho, which is noodles."

"Sounds yummy."

"With any luck, it won't disappoint. Why don't you fire up the briquettes and I'll meet you outside as soon as the marinade's ready?"

****

The lemongrass chicken was a hit. Maggie and Claire sat so close together that their forearms touched. And each time skin touched skin, a warmth spread through Claire like a smoldering fire.

Maggie swiped her lips with a paper napkin. "Delicious, Claire. I can't tell you how much I enjoyed the chicken. You must share the sauce recipe."

Claire winked. "It's my secret recipe, but I may be coerced into revealing its ingredients."

Maggie took Claire by surprise when she stood and rapped a steel fork against an aluminum cup. "Attention. Attention, please. How about a round of applause for our chef?"

Recruits and children hooted, hollered, and clapped their approval.

Red-faced, Claire did a mock bow and curtsy.

"What are you going to cook next, Claire?" Kimmy asked.

"Hmm. How about *Thit Nuong?*"

A crescendo of voices shouted "Yay!"

"Will you cook it for us today?" Kimmy asked.

Claire laughed. "Not today, kiddo. Maybe next week?"

Maggie whispered into her ear. "*Thit Nuong?*"

"It's a grilled pork dish. You'll love it."

****

After the kitchen sparkled clean and they were alone, Maggie sat down and patted the seat next to her.

"Take a load off, Claire. You worked your ass off today. I have something I want to show you."

Claire stared at a medium-sized manila envelope Maggie

had placed on the table top. "What's this? Instructions for a top secret mission?"

Maggie chortled. "You've been watching too many reruns of Mission Impossible, haven't you?"

"It's better than listening to the base radio, where they bleep out every other word of news reports. Or tuning in to the 'top forty' song station that is something out of the 1950s."

Maggie laughed. "We are a bit backward here. But seriously, consider this a present, of sorts.

Claire opened the envelope's flap and pulled out a stack of black-and-white photography stills. The first four were close-ups she'd taken of Kimmy the first day they'd met. Kimmy's forlorn expression exuded raw emotion and stark reality. Claire took a sharp breath. The next series of photos were long-range shots in the moments before Kimmy became frightened and darted off.

As if sensing Claire's unease, Maggie grabbed the remaining pictures and tried to cram them back into the envelope.

"I'm sorry, Claire. I overstepped my bounds in having them developed."

"No. That's not it. Kimmy looks so sad, so traumatized."

"Those photos are intense and thought-provoking. You should feel proud that you were able to capture Kimmy's true essence."

"I guess so." Claire flipped to another set of photos and burst out laughing. "These are new. I didn't take these."

"Oh, these are the ones Kimmy and I took. They're really just a bunch of silly shots, none as frame worthy as yours."

"I love silly shots and these take the cake!"

Claire spread the photos out on the table. In one, Kimmy's sticking her tongue out and making peace signs behind Maggie's head. In another, a close up, Maggie and Kimmy were cheek to cheek, mugging for the camera. Still another, the two were standing side by side making the shape of a heart with their fingers across their chests.

"They're outrageous. I love them. How did you manage

to develop the film?”

“I have an ‘in’ with our aerial logistics department. They develop a ton of reconnaissance photographs daily. To develop this roll was a treat for them. A break from the chaos. You’re not angry, are you?”

“How could I be?”

“Sometimes I can be impulsive.”

Claire rolled her eyes skyward. “Not you, Captain Margaret Anne Calder with an *e*.”

Maggie shouldered her hard. “Knock it off.”

Claire grinned and slid the photos back in the envelope. “Thank you, Maggie. And thank you, again, for the sightseeing tour yesterday. You’ve definitely made life on base exciting. I can’t wait for our next adventure.”

“Funny you should mention that.”

Claire cocked her head to the side. “Uh-oh. By the tone of your voice, it sounds like this might be trouble.”

“I promise it’s nothing too dangerous. Just a tad against base rules is all.”

“Well, now that you’ve piqued my curiosity, don’t leave me in suspense. Out with it.”

“What are your chances of sneaking out tonight? Maybe around midnight? It is Saturday, you know.”

Claire blanched. “Midnight!”

Maggie laughed. “Yes, Claire, as in the stroke of.”

“My mother always warned me that nothing of virtue goes on after dark.”

“Yeah, and I bet your mother always told you that she had eyes in the back of her head, too.”

Claire grinned. “Where are we going?”

“That’s a secret.”

“Sounds very cloak and dagger to me. I’m starting to believe that you’re becoming a bad influence.”

“You say bad influence like it’s a good thing.”

“Maybe it is.”

“Then that’s a yes?”

“Unless you hear dogs barking and whistles blowing. That means Bunsen has rounded up a posse.”

“Groovy. Then I’ll catch you on the flip side.”

“Wait. What should I wear?”

"An evening gown with pearls."

"Funny. I mean, do I have to wear my ARC uniform?"

"Jeans and a T-shirt will do."

"Can I bring my camera?"

"Not this time. It's a 'for your eyes only' kind of gathering. Besides, I thought you needed a change of scenery. And, it's the least I could do after you spoiled me with that scrumptious, home-cooked meal."

****

Claire's thoughts ran wild as she lay looking at the ceiling, counting down the minutes until she would see Maggie.

At five to midnight, she sat up and pulled aside the bedsheet. Clad in a T-shirt, jeans, and socks, she swung her legs over the cot's edge and flattened her feet on the canvas covered floor. When she attempted to stand, she winced and froze at the sound of the cot's rickety metal frame creaking. Damn it. Bunsen's sure to hear. And then she heard a grunt followed by someone snoring up a storm. Oh, thank God. Some background noise to mask her escape.

In one fluid motion, perfectly timed with the loud snoring, Claire rose and snagged her sneakers. She tiptoed across the distance separating her from the tent flap. To her luck, the last person in for the night hadn't secured the fabric ties. With ease, she slipped through the yawning gap.

She scampered a few yards away before taking the time to slip on her sneakers. She stood and looked around in the dark. She heard the soft putt-putt of the motorbike before homing in on the tiny beacon of light flickering from an area a block's distance from the sleeping quarters. She hurried toward the illumination. Toward Maggie.

"Glad to see you made it," Maggie whispered.

Claire hopped on the back of the motorbike and rested her hands on Maggie's hips. "I wouldn't have missed it for the world."

Maggie handed Claire a white helmet. "Best we wear these. Not sure what the roads are like and, with my light coloring, it'll make us less noticeable."

"Care to clue me in on where we're going?"

"Saigon."

Claire blinked. "Saigon? Isn't that far?"

"It's a bit of a jaunt, but well worth the ride."

"Is it...safe?"

Maggie touched Claire's hand. "Where we're going is totally safe. Trust me."

Claire strapped on the helmet. "I do trust you."

"Good. Hold tight."

There was something about escaping in the night, under a moonlit sky, that was so damn sexy. Claire tightened her grip and leaned against Maggie's back as if they were one. At that moment, Claire didn't care if they rode on for hours and never reached their destination. For her, the comfortable silence lulled her into a state she could only describe as pure ecstasy. Although it was too dark to make out much of the passing scenery, Claire imagined she saw flowering trees and lush tropical foliage in brilliant arrays of color flanking her on either sides of the path.

After a time, the motorbike slowed to a crawl and Maggie turned her head to the side so Claire could hear her. "We're close. I'm going to cut the headlight and glide the rest of the way."

When the motorbike came to a full stop, Claire checked out her surroundings. They were in a narrow alley that backed a cluster of storefront establishments that were closed for the night.

Claire slid off the bike. "Where are we?"

"One of Saigon's best-kept secrets."

Maggie stowed the bike behind a row of trashcans before reaching for Claire's hand. When Claire resisted, Maggie asked.

"What's wrong?"

"You're sure this is on the up and up?"

Maggie touched her shoulder. "Are you scared?"

"Not necessarily scared, but cautious. When I lived at the orphanage, venturing out once the sun set, especially if you were female, was taboo. If one was caught, there was strict punishment to endure."

"You are no longer a child, Claire, and I swear I would never expose you to a dangerous situation. There are no enemies here. Only friends."

Reassured, Claire followed Maggie to a brick building with a red-painted door. She rapped once, then twice, then three times. Not a second passed before the door opened a sliver, revealing soft yellow light emanating from within.

Maggie exchanged nods with whoever answered the door before the light snuffed out and the door opened wide to bid them entrance.

Once the door closed behind them, the light turned back on and Claire stood looking at a petite Vietnamese woman with warm brown eyes and a welcoming smile.

"Mai," Maggie said, enfolding the woman in a hug, "it's so nice to see you."

"Da, Maggie. It's been so long. Why have you stayed away?"

Maggie shrugged. "Busy, I guess."

Mai eyed her with a seemingly knowing look. "Beatrice says otherwise."

Maggie chuckled. "Beatrice doesn't know her ass from a hole in the ground."

Mai peered past Maggie's shoulder. "I see you've brought a friend."

"*Da.*"

"Welcome," Mai said.

"*Khong co gi,*" Claire replied. "It's a pleasure."

"Are we late?" Maggie asked.

"No. You're just in time. Follow me."

Mai led them down a dimly lit hall. As they progressed, Claire heard the steady thump, thump, thump of a musical beat. Claire yanked on Maggie's arm. "So, who's Beatrice?"

"A good friend. She's actually the guest of honor."

"I'm not following you."

"We're here for a going-away party. Beatrice's going-away party. She and Mai have been friends forever."

"Well, that explains the music, but I'm still unsure where here is."

"A nightclub, of sorts."

"A nightclub with no neon signs out front? Crunched in between stores?"

Maggie nodded. "A secret nightclub reserved for people

of our persuasion, if you catch my drift."

Claire felt her muscles relax. "Oh! That kind of night-club."

Maggie squeezed her hand. "Hang on to your britches, girl. You're about to enter lesbian heaven."

"Which is?"

"Women, women, women. Oh, and cheap booze and outdated music."

Mai shot Claire a knowing look before opening the door and ushering them inside.

The stark transformation from dim hallway lighting to vibrant, multicolored light made Claire's eyes tear up. Cigarette and marijuana smoke permeated the air. Claire noticed a huge overhead fan whirling at a fast speed to cut down on the thick haze. Standing beside Maggie, Claire scanned the large, rectangular-sized room. In a far corner stood a pool table surrounded by a group of women drinking beer while waiting their turn. In the opposite corner, a dance floor was packed with women gyrating to a honky-tonk song. To their right, women stood three deep at a wraparound bar eager to quench their thirsts.

"Wow," Claire said.

Maggie grinned. "You like?"

"Oh, yeah. It's a perfect place to get our groove on."

"The shuffleboard and dart areas are past the pool table."

"I love the diversity. So many women of different races and cultures."

"It's a melting pot here. That's what makes it so special. And it's far enough from Tan Son Nhut that no straight personnel would ever suspect. We can be ourselves here. Free from all the negative bullshit. Oh, over there in the corner are a few of my gal pals. But before we meet them, let's get ourselves a few cold brewskis."

As they waited in line at the bar, Claire twirled a swizzle stick. "Tell me about Beatrice."

"She's an ace. My right-hand gal when it comes to sneaking under the radar and having a rip-roaring good time. She's part of our intelligence staff on base."

"Intelligence?"

"Beatrice is sent on missions so top secret, even she doesn't know where she'll be at any given time." Maggie nodded to the bartender and held up two fingers. "*Hai bias.*"

"That must be exciting."

"I guess, if you like facing death at every turn. I must warn you, though. Beatrice is quite the handful."

When the beer arrived, Maggie handed Claire a long-necked bottle. "Cheers."

"Cheers," Claire replied and took a long swig.

Before Claire could inquire further about Beatrice being a handful, the music died, the lights dimmed, and hushed whispers disturbed the sudden silence.

Maggie snagged Claire's elbow. "Hurry. She's coming."

With Maggie in the lead, they crossed the dance floor to meet Maggie's friends.

"Sophie. Marcie. This is Claire."

Both women smiled and shook Claire's hand before motioning toward two empty bar stools. Sophie whispered, "Nice to meet you. We can talk more after the surprise."

Claire heard the sound of approaching footsteps and garbled conversation before the door separating the bar from the hallway opened. In an instant, the lights turned on and the crowd, in unison, shouted "Surprise!"

A woman in the doorway, presumably Beatrice, reeled backward and gripped the side door jambs to keep from falling. "Jesus, Mary, and Josephine! What the hell's going on?" she shouted.

"Gotcha! Gotcha! Gotcha!" Maggie screamed, amidst the hoots and hollers.

From the 'creamed in the face with a pie' expression on the woman's face, the surprise was a huge success.

"Beatrice!" Maggie shouted. "Over here!"

Semi-recovered from her shock, Beatrice made her way past well-wishers who took turns slapping her on the back and shaking her hand. Music again blasted through speakers and women flooded the dance floor.

Marcie popped the cork on a bottle of champagne and handed the frothing bottle to the guest of honor.

"Here's to you, Beatrice Ellis! You get the first swig."

Beatrice didn't hesitate. She opened her mouth wide and guzzled from the rim. All laughed as champagne foamed down her chin. She slammed the bottle onto the table and wiped her mouth with her sleeve.

"You're all damn bitches, you know that? Scaring a woman hours before she's off to save her country from murder, mayhem, and madness."

"We didn't want you to leave without a proper farewell," Sophie said.

"Yeah," Marcie chimed in. "You deserve it, Bea."

"I deserve a hot lovin' woman, that's what I deserve. And all this surprise shit's thrown my libido off track. Shame on you all."

Maggie piped in. "Don't bullshit us, Ellis. We know you have a honey in every port."

Beatrice scoffed. "Yeah, right."

Claire stepped back to watch Maggie's friends interact and take in their appearance. Sophie was tall, lean, and blonde whereas Marcie was short, a tad on the chubby side, and sported a close-cropped afro. Claire soon realized that once Beatrice entered a room, she became a commanding presence. Broad shouldered and muscular, Beatrice stood at a towering height of what Claire gauged to be over six feet. Her black, curly hair framed her square-jawed face. If it weren't for her warm, caramel-colored eyes and wide, contagious smile, Claire would've been easily intimidated by her loud, boisterous voice.

Claire soon learned that Beatrice wasn't one to miss a trick when she peered over Maggie's shoulder and asked, "And who's this pretty one hiding in the shadows?"

Maggie turned and reached for Claire's hand. She tugged twice before Claire moved forward. "Beatrice, let me formally introduce you to Claire McCallum. She's from upstate New York and works as an ARC interpreter on base."

Beatrice muscled past Maggie and extended her hand to Claire. "How-de-do, fair maiden."

"Oh, Christ, here we go with Bea oozing on the charm," Marcie said.

"So much for her libido being off track," Sophie mumbled.

To Claire's surprise, Maggie slid an arm around her waist and pulled her close. "Nice try, Ellis, but this fair maiden's with me."

Beatrice arched a brow. "Oh, is that so? Well, I'll be, Calder. I thought you were destined for a lone wolf existence."

Maggie shrugged. Beatrice again looked at Claire. "You must be some special lady to have caught this one's eye. What's it been, Maggie? Three years?"

Maggie laughed and waved to a waitress carrying a tray of shot glasses. "What kind of concoction are you serving?"

The waitress winked. "Mai's secret recipe."

"If it's good enough for Mai, it's good enough for us." Maggie took five shot glasses from the tray. "Keep it coming."

At one point, Sophie and Marcie took to the dance floor while Beatrice, Maggie, and Claire made small talk.

"When's your flight leave, Bea?" Maggie asked.

"At the crack of dawn."

Claire glanced at her watch. "Do you have far to go?"

"Nope. My base is close and Mai's arranged transport."

"Are you going to get in trouble for being drunk?"

Beatrice fixed Claire with a harsh stare. "Who says I'm drunk?" Beatrice watched Claire flop like a fish on a hook before bursting into laughter. "It takes a hell of a lot of booze to knock this gal on her keister. Besides, even if I end up hammered, I'll sleep it off during the flight."

A shrill whistle from across the room caught Beatrice's attention. "Charlize!" Beatrice shouted to a woman leaning against the bar and sucking on a toothpick. "Where have you been hiding?" Beatrice turned to Maggie and Claire. "If you ladies will excuse me, I have some unfinished business to attend to."

Maggie spread her arms wide. "Far be it from me to interfere with romance."

When they were finally alone, Claire blurted out, "What's with the 'she's with me' routine?"

Maggie scowled and took a swig of beer. "What do you mean?"

"I mean, since when are we a couple?"

Claire enjoyed watching Maggie squirm. "We are a couple. A couple of friends, right?"

"Are we?"

Maggie sighed. "Maybe a little more than that."

Claire felt a whoosh in her ears and a pounding in her temples. "How much more?" she whispered.

"To be honest? I'm intrigued by you. Intrigued by everything about you."

Surprised by Maggie's admission, Claire tried to laugh it off. "That's the booze talking, Calder. You know what they say about loose lips."

"It's not the booze. And I know all about loose lips sinking ships. That's why I joined the air force instead of the navy."

"I don't know what to say."

Maggie leaned in close enough for Claire to feel her soft breath against her cheek. "Say that you're as intrigued by me as I am you."

"I..."

"I'm not the only one, am I?" Maggie asked. "The only one who feels the tension between us? The sexual tension?"

Claire's body tensed. She reminded herself to remain calm, cool, and collected. Now that the moment she'd dreamt about, fantasized about, was finally here, she felt torn whether to play it safe or expose her soul.

She looked in Maggie's eyes, saw the intensity in her gaze, and threw caution to the wind. "Maggie, whenever I'm around you I feel energized, like a bolt of electricity is searing through my veins."

"For me, it's more like an irresistible urge to take you into my arms and kiss you."

Claire made a show of batting her eyelashes. "Would you settle for shaking it up with me on the dance floor, as a start?"

Maggie swept an arm in front of her. "After you."

****

Claire and Maggie be-bopped to a set of songs that began with "Rock Around the Clock," "The Locomotion," and a karaoke version of "The Night They Drove Old Dixie Down."

Maggie moved in close when the music wound down to a soft love ballad and the lights dimmed. "They're playing 'I'll Be Seeing You,' by Billie Holiday. She's my favorite singer in the whole, wide world. Will you slow dance with me?"

"I thought you'd never ask."

For a few panic-stricken moments, each fumbled for hand placement with Maggie's hands settling on her hips, and Claire draping her arms loosely on Maggie's shoulders. When they moved against each other, Claire's skin tingled. Every slight touch of their thighs grazing sent shockwaves of pleasure coursing through Claire. Talk about getting wet, she thought. She was there.

Claire kept her head lowered and tilted to the side so Maggie couldn't see her face. If the eyes really were the windows to the soul, Claire didn't want Maggie to see the depth of her emotion. And then, there was the heat of Maggie's breath against her throat. Claire felt lightheaded from the intermingled sensations.

Until the music abruptly stopped and bright lights flickered on and off. On and off. On and off.

"What the hell?" Claire pulled away.

"That's Mai's signal that party time's over."

"Right in the middle of a song?" Claire asked.

"It must be three. Even secret women's clubs have a closing time."

"But I'm so enjoying our dance."

Maggie grinned. "Me, too. Claire, can I..."

Beatrice ruined the moment by staggering up to Maggie, hoisting her up by her belt buckle, and flipping her over her right shoulder. "I love this woman!" Beatrice slurred. "She's a winner, she is! Always has my back!"

Maggie pounded hard on Beatrice's back. "Okay, sentimentality time's over. Put me down, you Amazon warrior."

Beatrice loosened her grip enough for Maggie to slide down and regain her footing.

"And you!" Beatrice said, pointing at Claire.

Claire cringed.

Beatrice had Claire wrapped in a bear hug before she could flee.

"You are a breath of fresh air! I'm counting on you to breathe life back into my Maggie. She's lived with her black heart long enough."

"Okay, okay. Enough already, Beatrice," Maggie said, wedging in and breaking their embrace. "Time to meet your transport."

"But I want to stay!" Beatrice whined.

"Nope. Time to go." Maggie motioned to Sophie and Marcie. "Girls, need a little help here seeing our dear friend out."

It took Maggie, Claire, and the girls twenty minutes to get Beatrice out Mai's front door to an awaiting rickshaw. Claire eyed the light, two-wheeled, one-seat vehicle and its two straw-hatted foot-runners lounging in the alley, smoking a joint.

"That contraption looks awfully rickety," Claire said.

"It's stronger than it looks. I'm glad to see that Mai requested two drivers. Beatrice is dead weight when she's had too much to drink."

"And the drivers? Can they be trusted as far as not revealing to anyone on base where Beatrice's been?"

"They're Mai's nephews and are sworn to secrecy. All's good. Which brings me to us. Are we all good, Claire?"

This time, Claire met Maggie's eyes and held fast. "As right as rain."

"Speaking of which..." Maggie extended her hands, palms up. "It's already starting to sprinkle. We're going to have a wet ride if we don't hurry back."

****

Maggie dropped Claire off at their initial meeting spot at ARC's base camp moments before dawn. She held the motorbike steady so Claire could dismount.

"I hope you're not going to get in too much trouble with Buns for staying out the entire night. I know how she likes all of her chickadees snuggled in their nest."

Claire yawned. "Oh, I don't intend to go back into the

sleeping tent this close to daylight. I'm going to hide out over there, near the showers."

"Good thinking. Especially since you're slurring a little."

Claire grinned. "Mai's secret recipe sure packs a punch."

Maggie laughed. "Or you're a lightweight when it comes to liquor."

"Guilty as charged. In any event, I had such a great time, Maggie. Your friends are outrageous. Especially Beatrice."

"Beatrice is, indeed, a force to be reckoned with."

"I look forward to spending more time with them. And with you, too."

Maggie winked. "Count on it."

Maggie had no sooner puttered away when Claire turned to see Bunsen barreling toward her.

"Why, you're up early, Ms. Bunsen. I guess you enjoy the mornings as much as I do."

"Hogwash. You're no early riser. I'll warn you once, Recruit McCallum. No special privileges just because you work for an officer. You better make up your mind if you want to abide by ARC's rules or receive a formal reprimand. I refuse to waste another minute of sleep waiting up for you."

Claire's face flushed beet red. "Yes, ma'am."

Damn, Claire thought, as she slinked to her cot in shame. Maybe Maggie could pull some strings with Bunsen and get permission to have her sleep at MSU. After all, it was where she spent most of her time, and she could be close to the orphans.

Chapter Ten

Still licking her wounds from Bunsen's burning reprimand, Claire made it a point to steer clear of her for the better part of the morning. She ate a cold bowl of oatmeal and half a banana before setting out for MSU's sector to help the other volunteers with coordinating activity time for the orphans. And, she hoped with any luck, she'd get to see Maggie, too.

After Maggie's confession on the dance floor at Mai's, Claire felt as if she were walking, no jumping, leaping, bounding on cloud nine.

A shout from behind made her pause.

George limped up to her wearing a reproachful expression.

"Not so fast, little lady. You're about as hard to find as a bear cub in winter. Where have you been the last few days?"

"Nowhere in particular. Just kick-ass busy over at MSU. I haven't had too much free time to kick back."

"I could've used your support the other day."

"Why?"

"Ping pong rematch."

"Oh? I didn't know one was planned."

"Last minute."

"Sorry."

"Oh, well, never mind," George grumbled. "I didn't win. That no good-for-nothing Dickey beat the shit out of me."

"Really?"

George spat. "Rest easy, Claire. A one-time win doesn't make Dickey the new champ. Kick-ass busy, huh?"

"Yeah. Can't you see I'm walking as if I rode a bronco bareback?"

George squinted his eyes and leaned in close. "You ain't fooling me, McCallum. I know that look."

Claire felt her heart skip a beat. "What look?"

"The look like you've got a friend."

"I have lots of friends."

"Oh no, little lassie. This friend is different. I can tell."

Claire tried to laugh off George's perceptiveness. "What are you now? A mind reader?

"Nope, but I recognize the gleam in your eyes and the pep in your step. You got a honey, or you're damn close to having one."

"I think you're getting daft in your old age."

George shrugged. "Deny it all you want, but I know what I see. You're in love."

Claire nudged him. "Stop being a pain in the ass, George."

"Sticks and stones may break my bones."

"Enough already, old man. Don't you have something better to do than make my life miserable?"

"Nope."

Claire eyed her watch. "Well, I do. Catch up later?"

"Sure, if your ass isn't too kicked by this secret lover of yours."

****

By mid-afternoon, Claire teetered on the verge of collapse. Her sweaty clothes clung to her body, and the knees of her jeans were muddy and grass stained. Activity time with the orphans had included relay races, hide-and-go-seek, and tag. And had lasted hours. The children were inexhaustible and unstoppable.

Claire sat on a low retaining wall to catch her breath and ease her aching muscles. Approaching footsteps made her look up.

"Damn, girl. You look like you've been mud wrestling. And lost," Maggie said.

"You could say that."

Maggie laughed. "I heard all about it from one of the gals. Here, I thought you'd like something to drink." She handed Claire an ice-cold bottle of Fresca from its base with its neck pointed towards Claire. The cap was already off so she could drink it. Claire scrunched her eyebrows. How weird. Then she got it. Maggie didn't want their fingers to touch. Whereas the night before they were free to express emotion, today any form of contact was expected to be minimal, at best. Don't want the rumor mills stirring.

Claire chugged half the bottle in one swig. She let out a stifled burp. "Thanks. Oh, my God, Maggie, it was horrible. A living nightmare."

"Looks like you need a nice hot shower and some R&R. And, I might know the ideal place to do both."

Claire scratched at a mosquito bite on the tip of her nose. "Is it within crawling distance?"

"A stone's throw, really. The female officers' building. That's where I bunk in a studio style apartment."

"Are civilians allowed in the officers' building?"

"Of course. Why do you ask?"

"There's so many rules around here, I couldn't help wondering if it's a no-no for officers to fraternize with the underlings."

Maggie laughed. "Underlings, huh? Is that how you see yourself?"

Claire shrugged. "It's not like volunteers have the true grit experience or rank of enlisted soldiers."

"Don't knock yourself, Chicken Scratch. You're true grit enough for me."

Maggie unlocked the apartment door, flipped on an overhead light, and stepped aside. "Ladies first."

Claire whistled. The studio consisted of a small living room, kitchenette, and a full-sized mattress without a headboard. She chuckled at the oversized posters Maggie had stapled to the walls. One was of Cheech and Chong, peeking out from behind a thick curtain of cannabis plants, another of Janis Ian lazing on a blue-suede divan, and a Janis Joplin facial shot with a cigarette dangling from her lips. "I love the décor."

"Spoken like a true hippie chick," Maggie teased. They shared a laugh. "Honestly, what do you think?"

"Small, but homey."

"Cramped as it may be, it does serve its purpose. The shower's always hot and window screens do wonders with keeping out the mosquitoes."

Claire sighed. "Oh, how I miss window screens."

"I know how you feel. I've done my time sleeping in tents. Too many gaps in the canvas and not enough air circulation."

"It's not all that bad. Of course, privacy is at a minimum, but everyone seems to get along."

Maggie leaned against a wall support. "You never complain, do you?"

"We live in the lap of luxury compared to how our troops fare through the day and night. And then there's the villagers..." Claire shuddered. "Every day and night spent in fear for their lives, foraging for food, fighting disease. It makes me sick."

"You amaze me, Claire."

"How so?"

"Your depth of feeling, of devotion, is breathtaking. Especially with the way you interact with the children."

"Being here is where I want to be, where I can serve my purpose of caring for others."

Claire squirmed beneath Maggie's intense gaze.

"So, are you ready?" Maggie asked.

"Ready?" Oh God, was that Maggie's indirect way of asking her to have sex?

Maggie's eyes gleamed. "For a shower, Claire. Are you ready for a shower?"

"Oh. Oh! Yes. That would be swell."

Maggie leaned in closer. "What did you think I meant?"

"I—Never mind."

Maggie opened a dresser drawer and pulled out a tan T-shirt, a pair of sweats, and a pair of socks.

"Here's some fresh clothes to change into. The bathroom's off to the right. You'll find towels and anything else you might need there, including a new toothbrush."

"Thanks."

"While you're showering, I'll try to scrounge up something for us to snack on."

Claire grinned. "That'd be groovy."

Ten minutes later, feeling clean and refreshed, Claire slid on Maggie's clothes. As Maggie was taller in stature, the sweats bunched about her ankles but the T-shirt fit like a glove. She finger-combed her hair and brushed her teeth before she gathered up her dirty clothes and damp towel and padded into the living room.

Maggie turned from the kitchen counter where she stood preparing a fruit tray.

"My, my. You look fresh as a daisy."

"And I feel like one, too."

"You can put your dirty clothes over there, in the hamper."

"Do you need any help?"

"There's a few types of cheeses in the fridge you can slice up, and a box of crackers in the cabinet. If you can do that while I take a shower, that'd be great."

"Sure thing."

****

Once the cheeses were sliced and the crackers spread around them in a circle, Claire took closer notice of her surroundings. She smiled when she spotted a portable, hi-fi stereo system sitting on a wooden end table with a stack of music albums lying on the floor beside it. Such artists as Janis Ian, Joan Baez, and Joni Mitchell graced the album covers.

Claire appraised Maggie's collection and grinned when she found a Billie Holiday album. "Here's to recreating a moment," she said, as she slid the album from its protective sleeve, placed it on the platter, and switched on the turntable. She bent so that she could place the needle on the third groove. After a brief hiss and crackle, Holiday's timeless voice resonated through the apartment singing the sentimental ballad, "I'll be Seeing You," the same song she and Maggie had danced to at Mai's.

Caught up in the moment, Claire closed her eyes, pressed the album to her chest, and became lost in the lyrics. To her surprise, Maggie came up behind her and placed her hands on her hips.

"An excellent choice," Maggie whispered.

Claire lost her grip on the album cover and, with a contented sigh, tilted her head backward so Maggie could nuzzle her neck.

"Mm. Listening to Billie here is so much better than in that crowded, smoke-filled bar you took me to."

"I agree. Shall we pick up where we left off?"

Claire turned to face her. "Let's," she murmured.

Moving as one, they became caught up in the song's slow, sensuous tempo and the closeness of their bodies. Claire's heart swelled with affection and her body throbbed with desire. She shivered when Maggie's hands skimmed across her lower back and hips.

"I want you, Claire," Maggie whispered. "I want you so damn much."

Suddenly, a pealing alarm resounded through the apartment and siren blasts belched from outdoor speakers.

Claire recoiled. "My God, what's that?"

"Med alert. Someone's injured. We better hurry."

****

Once outside, Claire saw Salvatore and a group of medics carrying three stretchers toward the surgical tent.

"What the hell happened?" Maggie shouted, walking beside them.

"Somehow, these GIs got separated from their unit during a VC ambush," Salvatore yelled back. "They ended up floundering around in the dark and stepping on a land mine."

"Jesus!" Maggie cried out. "How bad?"

Salvatore shifted his weight to offset the burden. "Depends on the amount of trauma and blood loss sustained."

"How did they make it to base?"

"One of the nurses saw a throng of villagers standing in bushes at the far end of the base. When she went to investigate, she found our guys lying on a food cart. The villagers must've wheeled them a great distance to get help."

"Where's Bosworth?"

"Already prepping for surgery."

"What can I do? Claire asked.

Maggie pointed to a medic securing a tourniquet to a soldier's thigh to staunch blood gushing from a gaping wound. "Looks like that medic needs some help."

Claire leapt into action. "I'm Red Cross. First-aid trained. How can I help?"

Grizzled and harried, the medic shouted, "Get on the opposite side of me. Make sure that our soldier's airway isn't constricted, and don't lose your hold on the tourniquet or he'll bleed out from the femoral artery."

"Got it." Claire knelt beside the injured soldier. His complexion was as pale as alabaster. His eyes were open, and his lips were moving, but no sound was coming out. Claire grabbed his hand. "Shh. Try not to speak, soldier. Everything will be okay. You made it to base safely. We have trained medical staff to help you and your buddies."

As Claire reached for the soldier's wrist to check his pulse, his body went limp. When Claire again looked at his face, his eyes had rolled upward in their sockets and his mouth had gone slack. She dropped her head to his chest to listen for a heartbeat. Hearing none, she placed her index and second finger against the carotid artery in his neck. No pulse.

"He's not breathing!" Claire yelled.

The medic glanced at the soldier. "I'll take over maintaining pressure to his thigh while you perform CPR! Now!"

Claire went into life-saving mode. As she had been taught, she pinched off the soldier's nose, tilted his chin upward to open his airway, and breathed into his mouth to inflate his lungs. She then clasped her hands together over the soldier's sternum and began compressions. The alternated series of breaths then compressions continued on and on and on, until she lost all sense of time. Adrenalin coursed through her veins, enabling her to continue CPR for what seemed an eternity. And, finally, the soldier gasped for air.

"I got him!" Claire cried.

The medic let out a weary sigh. "Thank Christ." With a free hand, the medic handed Claire a clear bottle with a valve on one end. "Do you know how to use a BVM?"

Claire took hold of the bag valve mask. "Yes."

"Good. Keep it handy, just in case you need to manually

resuscitate."

Claire's legs felt like rubber as she moved from a kneeling to a sitting position. Now that the emergency had passed, she was hit with a wave of fatigue that had her body quaking. He's alive. She'd done it! She'd helped save someone's life. She'd served a purpose.

Seconds later, two nurses came to the medic's aid and helped carry the soldier into the surgery tent. As they were going in, Maggie strode out. God, she looked awful, and Claire struggled to her feet to meet her.

"How did it go in surgery?" Claire asked.

Maggie unbuttoned her blood-stained shirt and peeled it off to the undershirt beneath. "Neither survived."

"Shit."

"One had a massive head wound and never regained consciousness. The other was pronounced DOA as soon as he got on the table. I guess it was their time of reckoning."

Claire blinked. "Did you say 'reckoning'?"

"I sure as hell did."

"But for what? They haven't done anything so horrible to deserve to be blown to pieces. They're victims, too."

"You think so, huh? Allow me to enlighten you to the truth. One of the nurses found extra food rations, extra clips of ammo, and half-filled water canteens stuffed in their backpacks."

"So?"

"The extra canteens had other soldiers' names stenciled on them that didn't match with our guys' dog tags."

Claire's stomach constricted. "You think they went AWOL?"

"I do. I had Salvatore check with headquarters. No radio call came in alerting anyone of the VC ambush. That's strict protocol. No radio call, no way of sending out reinforcements or air transport. I think those bastards got cold feet when the going got tough, snagged what they could, and took off on foot. What a bunch of cowards."

"I'm sure panic is a normal reaction."

Maggie glared at her. "No good soldier panics. They're a disgrace to the military. If they'd survived, they would've been court-martialed. Gutless bastards."

Claire was stunned by Maggie's reaction and biting words. "You sound so bitter."

"I am bitter."

"But they're just kids, barely old enough to shave."

"They knew the risks."

"Two thirds of our military forces are draftees, for God's sake!"

"Well then, you should feel real proud if the last draftee survives. He'll be sorry once Leavenworth gets hold of him and he's put behind bars. He'll be the example that the military doesn't tolerate deserters."

Claire felt her voice choke up. "Maggie, this isn't you talking. This can't be you talking."

"Oh, you bet your sweet ass it's me talking. I bet these scumbags hid in the shadows while brave souls stood their ground and fought to their death. They didn't have the decency to radio in. Who knows how many lay injured that could've been saved?" Maggie spat on the ground.

"But—"

Maggie glared at her. "Don't tell me you're a bleeding heart, McCallum."

Claire felt as if she were under attack for showing empathy. "I'm only saying that no one knows how they're going to react under—"

"Bleeding hearts are weak, too."

Claire felt as if she'd been slapped in the face. "I don't like what you're implying."

Maggie stared at her with a look of distaste. "You don't have to. In fact, you don't have to like anything about me."

Run. Claire heard a voice deep inside her urge. Run away. Get as far away as you can. With effort, she found her voice. "I made a mistake. I shouldn't have come."

On unsteady legs, Claire turned and walked away. Her departure was met with silence.

****

With tears streaming down her cheeks, Claire made her way back to ARC. And, to her chagrin, saw George pacing outside her sleeping tent.

"Claire, thank God. I was beginning to lose hope that I'd get to see you before I left."

Claire sniffled, wiped her face on her shirtsleeve, and hoped George wouldn't notice that she'd been crying.

"Going where?"

"Home. I just got word that my discharge date got moved up. I leave in the morning."

George's admission hit Claire like a ton of bricks, and she swayed on her feet. "No."

"I don't have much say in it, little lady. Time for this old buzzard to head back to that sleepy old mining town outside of Reading, Pennsylvania."

A searing sensation roiled in her gut, like she'd been stabbed. "But you're my friend. My one true friend."

George guffawed. "I find that hard to believe."

Try as she might to keep her composure, fresh tears welled in her eyes and her upper lip twitched.

"Hey. What's wrong? You look like you just got word that Christmas is cancelled."

"I..."

George grabbed her hand and led her to a picnic table. "Rest your laurels here, Claire." He yanked a tattered handkerchief out of a back pocket and blotted her eyes. Claire wasn't sure how long it took for her bout of tears to subside, but the whole time George sat next to her, holding her hand and lending emotional support without ever saying a word.

Finally, she calmed down enough to tell him about the injured soldiers in MSU and Maggie's suspicion they were deserters.

George scratched his stubbly chin. "It's quite possible they went AWOL. The horrors of the jungle can make the most courageous of men turn yellow. You said only one survived?"

Claire nodded. "He was still alive last I saw him."

"Well then, his truth will eventually be told. And, as deemed, he'll have to accept the consequences of his actions."

"George, what do you think of someone who deserts a military unit during an attack?"

"It's not for me to judge. War does crazy things to people.

Messes with your head in a way that can turn the meek psychotic, and the hard-hearted into blubbering idiots."

"So, is it wrong for me to feel empathy for him?"

"Hell, no. You're human. And, as the old adage goes, to err is human. Remember that night when you asked me what was my worst mistake?"

Claire nodded.

"I think now might be a good time to tell you about it. It happened on Sunday, December seventh, nineteen forty-one."

Claire felt the blood drain from her face. "Pearl Harbor? You were at Pearl Harbor?"

"Yup."

Claire voice hitched. "I mean, I know the Japanese attacked our naval base in Honolulu, but I've never met anyone, never had the opportunity to talk with anyone who had first-hand knowledge."

"Long story short, thousands of our armed forces and civilians were lost to the air strike. But you don't want to hear the short version, do you?"

"I only want to hear what you're willing to tell about the events. I don't want to drum up bad memories for you."

"Life's a bad memory, lassie, when you serve your country over consecutive tours. Just some memories eat at you worse than others. Back then, I was an aircraft mechanic. The attack began just before eight on a bright, clear, beautiful Sunday morning. The Lord's Day, right? I'd spent the night playing poker, drinking hard, and losing a bundle, so I overslept and missed roll call. Until the sound of bombs rattled my cot so hard, I came to with a start and scrambled into action mode."

George paused for just a moment. "We were caught by surprise, totally with our pants down. As you can you imagine, utter chaos took hold. Christ, what a fire storm. Later, we learned that the Japanese air strike was conducted in three stages: first, to take out as many people and equipment as possible; second, to target our aircraft carriers; and third, our battleships. We took a heavy beating, both in casualties and transport. To this day, I can't get rid of the stench of burnt skin from my nose or the sound of howling from all those poor souls who were too far gone to save."

"It's a miracle you survived," Claire said.

"I only survived because I overslept and didn't report to my station, which ended up being Ground Zero."

"It doesn't matter what you were doing, George. You made it out of the storm."

"While others perished."

After a few moment of silence, Claire asked. "Is that why you kept re-enlisting?"

George nodded. "Yup. I wanted to make right what I'd done wrong."

"And have you succeeded in righting those wrongs?"

"To a point. I sleep a little better now. I healed and carried on. Protecting your country is a service I've never taken lightly."

"I'm glad you shared your story with me. It must be awful to live with the memories."

"Darlin', you can't survive shitholes like World War II, or Korea, or Vietnam without it carving a wound deep in your heart. Over the years, I've learned that if you keep all that pain bottled up, it'll fester and gnaw at you from the inside out. Talking about the atrocities of war soothes the pain. Makes it bearable. Does that make sense?"

"It does."

George glanced at his watch and stood. "Time for me to go and pay my last respects to a few other worthy souls." He thrust out his hand. Instead of taking it, Claire flung her arms around George's neck and pulled him close. "What am I going to do without you, George Waldron?"

"You're going to write me letters and, once in a while, hit the MARS tent so I can hear your lovely voice. When you've completed your duty here, I want you to return to the States and search me out. I meant what I said about operating my own VFW post in my hometown. We can catch up and rehash old times over a beer or two."

Claire smiled despite her upset. "Or three, or four."

"Hah! You know me too well, McCallum."

Bunsen's voice interrupted their moment. "I thought I heard your voice, ARC Recruit McCallum."

Claire groaned. "Bunsen is such a buzzkill."

George chuckled. "You better go before she busts a gasket. Besides, I hate long, drawn-out goodbyes."

Claire loosened her grip and looked deep into George's eyes. "Then we'll leave it with see you soon?"

"Count on it."

Chapter Eleven

Claire awoke with a start from a nightmare. In the dream, she and Maggie were tethered by a thin rope, dangling from a steep precipice. No matter how hard Claire tried, she couldn't get her footing on the craggy rocks. Her fingers and palms were scraped and bleeding. Sweat clouded her vision and burned her eyes. The altitude made it difficult for her to breathe.

"I don't think I can make it, Maggie," Claire panted.

Maggie looked down at her with contempt. "You need to keep going, Claire. Don't be weak."

"It's my legs. They're not strong enough to support my weight. We've been climbing for hours and seem no closer to reaching the top. It's useless."

Maggie sighed. "Then you leave me with no choice."

Lightning fast, Maggie pulled a long, serrated knife from a leather sheath attached to her utility belt.

"What are you doing?"

"You've become a burden to me. A burden I need to rid myself of."

Maggie sliced into the rope, and Claire fell backwards, clawing at the air, eyes bulging, and mouth agape in a choked scream. She woke before she hit bottom.

"Hey, Claire," Quincy whispered a short distance away. "Are you okay?"

Claire wiped sweat from her forehead and sat up. "Yeah. I think so."

"Bad dream?"

Claire shuddered. "You could say that."

"You overslept. Better hurry, or you're going to be late for duty."

Claire groaned and fell backward onto the mattress. The last thing she wanted to do was return to MSU and face Maggie. But if she stayed in ARC's sector, Bunsen would be up her ass wanting to know her business. Claire needed to hide out somewhere. Somewhere no one would think to look.

In a daze, Claire dressed and left the sleeping tent. She stopped dead in her tracks when she spotted Maggie waiting for her at the picnic bench she and George had sat at the night before.

"You didn't show up for work detail this morning," Maggie said.

"What's it to you?"

"Can we talk?" Maggie asked.

When Claire tried to sidle past her, Maggie blocked her way.

Claire balled her hands into fists. "I don't think you want to do that."

"Claire, please. We need to talk."

"Talk is cheap, Maggie. Besides, last night you were crystal clear in voicing your opinion of me. No further explanation is needed."

Maggie gripped Claire's wrist for a brief second before Claire yanked it away.

"Claire, last night I was upset by what I'd experienced and took my frustration out on you. I want to make it right between us. Will you give me the chance?"

Claire rolled her shoulders and looked away.

"If not for me, please do it for the orphans, for Kimmy. Right this moment, she's waiting for you back at MSU. She's made you something special. She's been working on it for hours."

Claire seethed. "How dare you use Kimmy and the others as pawns? I won't fall for it. Not for one second."

Maggie held up her hands. "I'm sorry. I'm sorry. I just don't want the children to suffer for my bad behavior. I was hoping that you could spend the entire day with them and not have to set eyes on me until my workday's finished. Then, I thought we could go to our special spot. Once there, I promise to explain why I'm bitter and why certain circumstances have made me this way."

Maggie's pleading look tore at Claire's firm resolve but she held fast and refused to break under pressure. Finally, Claire said. "I'll think about it."

Maggie's eyes remained deadlocked on hers. "Think hard. It's important."

****

When Claire arrived at MSU, she found Kimmy seated on their favorite bench, swinging her legs back and forth.

"Hi, kiddo. What are you doing here sitting all by your lonesome?" Claire asked in Vietnamese.

"I wanted to give you a present before school starts."

Claire feigned surprise. "A present? For dear little old me?"

Kimmy nodded and reached for something on the bench beside her. "Now, close your eyes and don't peek."

"If I close my eyes, you're not going to cherry-on-top me again, are you?"

Kimmy clutched her belly and giggled. "Nooooo. You are so funny."

"Yeah, yeah. I'm a regular riot. Okay, I'm game. Lay it on me."

Claire closed her eyes and opened her hand, palm up. She felt something light settle against her skin.

"You can open your eyes now, Claire," Kimmy said.

Claire gasped. The present was an origami lei. Kimmy had carefully folded each colored piece of paper into a flower and then twined them together with thin rope to make a necklace.

"Wow, Kimmy. That is so, so *xing đep*. Beautiful. Thank you."

"I made it special for you because I think you, Claire, are beautiful."

Overcome with emotion, Claire held out her arms and Kimmy leaned into her embrace.

Eager to show her appreciation, Claire said. "I've got an idea. How about we teach the others how to make origami shapes after reading class? I bet they'd love it! And then, I'll make everybody PB and J sandwiches."

"Yay!" Kimmy shouted. "PB and J! PB and J for all!"

As promised, after morning studies and arts and crafts, Claire prepared PB&Js for the children for lunch. Afterwards, they were permitted to play in the activity yard until shower time. Later, tuckered out from play, Kimmy found Claire lazing in a hammock, and climbed in beside her with a story book in her hand.

"Will you read me a story, Claire?"

Claire eyed the book. Sleeping Beauty. "Sure thing, kiddo." By the time she'd reached the point in the fairy tale when Prince Charming kneels to kiss Sleeping Beauty, Kimmy was out like a light, snoring. Claire closed the book, slid it against her thigh, and dozed for the remainder of the afternoon.

****

Once Kimmy set off for the showers with the other orphans, Claire made her way to the front of MSU. She found Maggie seated on the motorbike, waiting. Maggie tried to smile but it came out more as a grimace.

"I wasn't sure you'd show up," Maggie said.

"That makes two of us."

"Hop on."

As they rode along dirt-patched roads, Claire didn't feel any sense of exhilaration at being with Maggie. Instead of wrapping her arms around her waist, Claire held on to the seat's curved back bar. When they reached the base of the mountain they dismounted and trudged the rest of the way to the top in silence and with hands apart. Claire looked up at the sky. Thick black clouds churned in the distance. Claire shivered at the noticeable drop in temperature. Looked like trouble was brewing. This better be quick. Maggie motioned for Claire to sit and, without any prompting on Claire's part, spoke.

"Her name was Cassandra, but I called her Cassie. She was a raven-haired, blue-eyed beauty, a fireball of emotion. She never backed down from a challenge, no matter how crazy it sounded. She was a free spirit, a rebel always with a cause, and I fell madly, hopelessly in love with her."

"How did you meet?"

"Five years ago, during air support and logistical training on Nha Trang, another U.S. operated air base in South

Vietnam. We were opposites from the get-go. Whereas I preferred my feet firmly planted on solid ground coordinating air missions, Cassie loved to be airborne, scoping out vulnerable areas of attack from above."

"How did you keep your relationship a secret?"

"Oh, there are ways. Stolen kisses here and there. Little gaps in time where we could sneak away. Let's just say that we became quite resourceful in selecting areas on base to spend intimate time together."

Claire felt an irrational pang of jealousy. "By intimate, do you mean that you took her here? To the mountain top?"

Their eyes met. "No. This place is ours and ours alone."

Claire heard the low, steady rumble of thunder. Maggie didn't seem to be aware of the approaching storm or she didn't care.

"What happened to her?" Claire asked.

Maggie sucked breath through clamped teeth. "On a routine reconnaissance mission, a ground-to-air missile struck Cassie's aircraft, forcing the crew to parachute out. Being lead commander, Cassie made sure the five crew members jumped first before she sent out a distress signal and then followed suit. The problem with that is, in the time it took her to send out the mayday call, the plane had traveled a great distance away from where the other crew members landed safely in a rice paddy. When Cassie did jump, she landed in enemy territory."

"Oh, my God. You mean the Viet Cong captured her?"

Maggie nodded. "And they did unspeakable things to her."

"Maggie, if it's too painful to—"

"No. The point I want to make is from the condition of Cassie's body when found by our search and rescue team, it was determined that she endured great physical agony. For her body to have sustained that much trauma, she had to have kept silent to the end."

"Cassie is a true American hero."

"After her death, I totally closed in on myself. I became bitter, cold-hearted. I even wore a black heart pendant around my neck to let everyone know to keep the fuck out of my way. But then..."

"Then what?"

"Then I saw you, and my self-imposed world of isolation and bitterness crumbled."

Claire's heartbeat quickened.

"Ever since we met, I haven't been able to think about anything but you," Maggie said. "I felt as if I was finally breaking through the darkness. And then I went and ruined it."

Claire kept silent.

"Last night, I said things I shouldn't have, but I want you, need you to understand why I reacted that way. When I learned that those soldiers had abandoned their post, I snapped. Cassie would've never done that. Cassie died for people like that. I wanted to see justice served. I realize now, I was wrong. That I've been wrong for a long time. That my black heart hasn't enabled me to feel empathy or compassion. I need to let go of the anger before it eats me up inside. I need to start over with my life. And I so want to start over with you."

"Maggie."

Before Claire could speak further, a blinding bolt of lightning slashed across the night sky followed by a ground-breaking rumble of thunder. A split second later, the sky released a torrential downpour.

"Damn it!" Maggie shouted. "I thought we had time."

"Should we make a run for it?"

"No way. It's too steep of a grade to descend, and it's already mudding up. We'd break our necks trying to get down."

"Then what the hell are we going to do?"

"Find shelter." Maggie grabbed Claire's hand and yanked her to her feet. "I know a place that'll keep us dry until the storm passes."

Hunched over to protect her face from the pelting rain, Claire trailed behind Maggie along the mountain's upper shelf. Twice she stumbled and twice Maggie was there to steady her.

When they came upon a small wooden structure, Maggie yanked on the door. It gave way with a screech and they collapsed inside.

They sat side by side, soaked to the skin, catching their breath.

"What is this place?" Claire croaked.

Maggie wiped her shirtsleeve across her face. "It's an abandoned sentry post."

"Will it hold?"

"It damn well better."

Claire shivered. "I'm scared."

"Of what?"

"Being sucked into the maelstrom. One night, when I was a child, a monsoon flared up without warning in the middle of the night. Caretakers at the orphanage yanked us from our beds and herded us to the basement. All I can remember is huddling together with the other children in the darkness and listening to the godawful keening sounds of the wind and the splintering of wood. When it was over, a section of the orphanage roof had been ripped away. It was the section that covered the sleeping area. We'd barely escaped with our lives."

Maggie pulled her close. "How horrible for you. But that's not going to happen this time, Claire. Not on my watch."

Maggie flicked on her pocket flashlight. She spotted a worn wool blanket and used it to cover Claire about the shoulders.

For a while, neither spoke. Instead, they listened to the incessant pounding of the rain and the banshee wail of the wind.

"Maggie. I understand why you reacted the way you did last night. I understand your loss. It is all consuming. I, too, have loved and lost."

"Your brother?"

Claire nodded. "My twin brother. His name was Minh."

"Will you now tell me about him?"

"We were inseparable. Like two peas in a pod. We were orphaned at birth, and lived in a group home until we were ten. That's when the home was attacked by insurgents and burned to the ground. Minh and a handful of others didn't survive. They were trapped within the flames."

Maggie shuddered. "Oh dear, sweet Jesus."

"I blamed myself for years that it was my fault Minh died. That if I had gotten to him sooner, he would still be alive."

"It's not your fault, Claire."

"I know that now, but back then, I was a child. The months following Minh's passing did little to ease my grief. I no longer viewed the world through rose-colored glasses. No longer took delight in the most simplest of life's pleasures. I suffered from horrific nightmares. If it weren't for my soon-to-be adopted parents love and support, I don't think I would've survived. The pain was too deep. Too raw. When their tour of duty ended, they took me back to the states and adopted me. They wanted to offer me a better life."

"Did they?"

"Oh, yes. But the memories still haunted me. So, I came back."

Maggie squeezed Claire's hand. "I'm so happy that you did."

"That's why when I met Kimmy, I was so drawn to her."

"She reminded you of yourself?"

"Yes."

A few beats passed.

"Wait," Maggie said. "Do you hear that?"

"Hear what?"

"That's just it. I hear nothing. I think the storm's let up."

Maggie rose to her knees and peeked through a gap in the shed's wood siding. "Hot damn. Storm clouds are still rolling in, but there's a break in the rain. We should go now, while we have the chance."

Claire frowned. "Do we have to? I kind of like hanging out with you, riding out a storm together. It's sort of romantic."

"Yeah, until Salvatore sets off looking for us with a search party. It's late and we've been gone a while. It's only a matter of time before we're missed."

"Ugh."

Maggie stood and bent to offer Claire a hand. "C'mon."

Maggie and Claire retraced their steps across the mountain

top to where they had originally made their ascent. Maggie took a step forward and slipped. "Damn it!"

"What's wrong?"

"As I suspected, it's a mud patch. It's going to be a slippery slope down on foot."

"What'll we do?"

"The only thing we can do. We're going to have to descend on our asses, using our hands and feet to maintain traction."

Claire gawked at the mud that caked Maggie's boots up to mid-calf.

"I prefer my mud baths at a spa, Maggie."

Maggie chuckled. "Desperate times call for desperate measures, my dear. I'll go down first, with you close behind. If I lose control, don't try to stop me."

Claire bit her lip.

"Believe me, Claire. If there was another way. I'd be the first to take it."

"Okay. Let's do it."

Claire cringed as slick, oozing mud and loose grass wormed its way under her clothes and into private places that rarely saw the light of day. With every rumble of thunder, Maggie moved faster. Claire matched her motion for motion until, with huge sighs of relief, they reached bottom.

They hopped on the motorbike and sped back to MSU seconds before another onslaught of rain fell.

Beneath MSU's overhead sector lights, Maggie and Claire appraised each other.

"Jesus, Claire! You look you were dipped in a vat of chocolate."

"And you look like you were rolled in monkey turds."

"Ha. Ha."

Claire wrung her hands. "Buns is sure to kill me now. Not only did I break curfew, but I look like something the cat dragged in."

"Buns doesn't have to see hide nor hair of you until morning, Claire."

"How do you figure that?"

"You're going to stay overnight with me, at my place."

"At your place? If someone sees us, the rumor mill will

explode with sexual innuendos."

Maggie grinned. "Maybe some of them might come true."

Claire held Maggie's smoldering gaze. "Maybe so."

"I'll go in first to make sure the coast is clear, by that I mean the hallways. If they are, I'll switch the lights on and off as your signal to haul ass." Maggie pointed to the Officer's Building. "My room is on the far left, second floor. Got it?"

"Aye, Aye, Captain."

Five minutes later, Claire got Maggie's all clear cue and sprinted to the building's side entrance. She took the interior steps two at a time until she reached the second floor. She opened the door a fraction of an inch. No sign of anyone. She darted down the hall.

Suddenly, an arm snaked out from an open doorway and pulled her inside.

Claire let out a small squeak.

"Shh, woman. It's me," Maggie whispered.

Once inside, Maggie locked the door and dimmed the lights.

She turned to find Claire standing inches behind her.

"I think you have some explaining to do, Captain Calder."

"I do?"

"Uh-huh. I have a sneaky suspicion that you planned all this."

Maggie smiled. "Planned a monsoon that trapped us in an abandoned shed and left us in danger of our lives? And then had us sliding by the seat of our pants down a muddy embankment?"

"No. I'm talking about the sexually charged, all hot and bothered part that's going to make me bust an artery if you don't do something about it."

Maggie slid her hands onto Claire's hips and drew her close.

"What would you like me to do?" Maggie asked.

"Kiss me."

"Hard or soft?"

"Feel free to mix it up. Just do it. Damn it."

Maggie kissed her with an intensity that left them both breathless. And, in that moment, time stood still. Claire absorbed Maggie's heat and her passion surged.

Maggie alternated between soft, feathery kisses and deep, longing thrusts of her tongue. "Do you like that?" she asked, tracing Claire's lips and jawline with an index finger.

"Oh, yes. More."

"More, huh? How much more?"

Claire reached for Maggie's hand and placed it in between her breasts, at the bra clasp. "Why don't you start here and work your way down from there?"

Maggie moaned. "Claire McCallum, you are a minx, and a dirty little minx at that. How about we continue this conversation in the shower?"

****

With her back pressed against the cool shower wall and her body wet beneath a cascade of warm water, Claire watched Maggie rub a bar of soap between her hands until it lathered. Her breath hitched when Maggie leaned in for a long, passionate kiss before caressing her neck and shoulders with her foamy fingers.

"You are so beautiful, Claire. I so want to touch you everywhere."

Claire arched forward. "Yes."

At Claire's urging, Maggie stroked her nipples in a circular motion until her pink nub hardened before trailing downward, across her stomach to cup her warmth.

Claire responded to Maggie's touch in a way that made her entire body quake with desire. Her guttural moans of pleasure shocked even her. Oh, Lord. Maggie was going to get her off right here in the shower. Would screams echo in such a small space? Would anyone besides Maggie hear her?

"Claire?" Maggie asked.

"Hmm?"

"I want to do this right. Take my time with you. Discover every hidden inch of you. Not take you in a shower because we're half crazed with lust for each other. Do you understand?"

"Yes."

They quickly rinsed and toweled off, and hurried to the bed.

Now snuggled in a warm, naked embrace beneath a tie-dye patterned blanket, Claire opened herself up to Maggie in a way she'd only fantasized about. No part of her body was off limits and each delighted in the other's touch.

"God, this feeling of skin against skin. It's electric," Claire said.

"I want to taste you, Claire. Make you cry out for me over and over again."

Claire spread her legs. "Hurry, Maggie. I can't hold out much longer."

Maggie went down on her with an intensity that had Claire bucking against her eager mouth and moaning in ecstasy. When Maggie sensed Claire was close to coming, she moved up to eye level. Lips on lips and clit on clit, they rode the wave of passion to a glorious release that left them sweat-slick and gasping for breath.

As they lay in each other's arms, Claire was the first to speak. "Wow."

Maggie stroked Claire's moist mound. "You can say that again."

"Wow."

Maggie laughed and kissed the tip of her head.

"You were incredible, you know. Insatiable."

Claire cheeks burned at the way Maggie stared at her body.

"I've never acted so free and uninhibited. So out-of-my-mind crazed. Maggie Calder, you bring out the wild animal in me."

"That explains the guttural roars I heard."

Claire lowered her head "You're embarrassing me."

"I don't mean to. It's just that what we shared is so special. Although it took a monsoon to finally get us together, it was sure worth the wait."

"And you aren't disappointed?"

Maggie tilted Claire's chin upward so they could look at each other.

"Why would I be disappointed?"

"Compared to you, I don't have much experience."

"Experience has nothing to do with it, Claire."

"And then there's the way you look, the way you carry yourself. Hell, everything about you is magnetic."

Maggie laughed. "Now look who's embarrassing who. I hate to disappoint you, but my conquests are few and far between. As you're beginning to realize, I'm quite selective when it comes to opening my heart and baring my soul. The truth is, what we shared was much more than sex. It had to do with feeling. True feeling. I care about you, Claire. More than I thought I would so soon."

"Is that a bad thing?"

"Only if you don't share the same sentiment."

"You know I do."

"I'm glad. Are you hungry?"

"Starved."

Claire dozed while Maggie brewed a fresh pot of coffee and toasted a few slices of rye bread.

Now, seated next to each other on the bed, Maggie said, "I propose a toast." Maggie chuckled. "Excuse the pun."

"What'll we toast to?"

"New beginnings and fairy-tale endings."

Claire looked into Maggie's eyes. Her heart was pounding so hard, it throbbed in her temples. "You mean falling in love and living happily ever after?"

Maggie leaned in for a kiss. "I mean just that. Or does that frighten you?"

Claire puffed out her bottom lip. "I don't frighten easily."

"Hm. We'll see."

Chapter Twelve

December, 1974

When Claire saw Maggie exit the MSU tent, she raced over and gripped her elbow like a vice.

"Ouch, Claire. That hurts."

"You're late. The show's about to begin."

Maggie grimaced. "Damn. I forgot. I've been ass-deep in paperwork."

"It's Christmas Eve, for Pete's sake."

Maggie stopped and glared at her. "War doesn't stop for holy days, Claire."

Claire loosened her hold. "I'm sorry. You're right. It's just that the children have worked so hard, and they're so looking forward to this."

Claire pointed to one of twenty folding chairs set up on the grass in rows of five.

"You're going to have to sit in the back row, behind the volunteers."

"Where are the children?"

"In the activity tent, waiting for my cue."

Maggie flashed her a weak smile. "Then don't let me keep you a minute longer."

Claire pressed an open hand, palm inward, to her chest, a sign they'd earlier agreed would stand for I love you, before standing before the audience. She cleared her throat. "Good evening and Happy Holidays, recruits and military staff! It's my pleasure to introduce Tan Son Nhut's very own merry band of carolers to bring good tidings to all in this most joyous of seasons." The audience clapped and cheered.

"And so, without further ado..." Claire undid the flaps on the tent and motioned inside.

In single file, twelve children, dressed in long white shifts with red satin bows sewn at the neck, exited the tent.

Each carried a lighted red candle. Without any prodding on Claire's part, they lined up before their audience with the taller children in the back and smaller children in front. Kimmy, the youngest, stood right smack in the middle. When the applause died down, Claire raised her hands and whispered, "On the count of three, children. One. Two. Three."

Together and in perfect harmony, the children sang "Silent Night" in English and then followed it up with five additional yuletide carols sung in Vietnamese. After they were finished, there wasn't a dry eye in the crowd.

Claire hung back while the audience made a show of hugging and kissing each child, and handing out presents that ranged from checker sets to game cards, and from hula hoops to jump ropes Maggie had ordered from the mainland. Kimmy squealed in delight when one of the recruits presented her with a colored pencil and stencil set.

Once gift giving was over, Claire handed out steaming mugs of hot chocolate and shortbread cookies.

Maggie moved beside her. "What a most blessed night."

"Amen."

****

As soon as the apartment door closed, Maggie swept Claire into her arms and spun her around.

"Whoa, there," Claire said. "Slow down. You're making me queasy."

"My God, Claire. The children were fabulous!"

Claire beamed. "Weren't they? I wish I could've taught them more songs in English, but we didn't have enough time."

"Silent Night was, indeed, the ultimate show stopper."

Claire took a hard look at Maggie. Saw the dark circles under her eyes and her furrowed brow. "Are you okay?"

"I will be."

"Would you like a drink? I've made homemade eggnog."

Maggie stroked Claire's hair. "My God, woman. You think of everything."

"I wanted tonight to be special."

"It was."

Maggie sagged into a dinette chair and covered her face with her hands.

Claire knelt beside her. "Oh, babe. I'm so sorry that you carry so much responsibility. It must be exhausting."

When Maggie raised her head, Claire saw tears in her eyes.

"Do you want to talk about it?" Claire asked.

Maggie sniffled and pushed back from the table. "No. Tonight is Christmas Eve. Tonight, we honor peace, love, and charity and dream of a much better world. And tonight, I'd like to give you something near and dear to my heart."

Maggie stood and moved toward her dresser. She opened its top drawer, pulled out a slim, elongated box, and placed it in Claire's hands.

"I'd intended to give you this on New Year's Eve, but after tonight, I couldn't wait any longer."

"What is it?"

"A promise."

Claire's body tingled.

"Go ahead, Claire. Open it."

Claire removed the lid and gasped in surprise. Set atop a bed of black satin lay a red ruby pendant attached to a thin, gold chain.

"Well, what do you think?" Maggie asked.

"It's exquisite."

Maggie lifted the necklace and motioned for Claire to turn around. Claire turned and lifted her hair so Maggie could secure the clasp at her neck. "Claire, I want you to have this as a symbol of my undying love for you. It's a promise to a future together. That is, if you accept."

Speechless, Claire wrapped Maggie in a fierce embrace.

"Is that a yes?" Maggie whispered against her throat.

"Yes! Yes! Where did you get it?"

"From my grandmother. My grandfather gave it to her as a promise, and she gave it to me upon her deathbed. For years I wore it until I replaced it with the black heart. But now, the black heart is gone and the ruby rests with the woman I want to share my life with. Not a bad start to a new year and, hopefully, a cease fire?"

Claire kissed Maggie.

"I love you, Maggie. I love you so much."

"And the fairy tale continues, my sweet. And do you know what the best part is?"

"Hmm?"

"Kimmy is going to be part of it."

"What do you mean?"

"I mean the three of us together, forever. Like the Three Musketeers. All for one and one for all."

Claire took a deep breath and let it out in short bursts. "You mean adoption? We can adopt Kimmy?"

Maggie nodded. "I know it's been on your mind from day one. And, not long after, I too harbored the same wish. Kimmy knows us. Trusts us. Loves us. The thought of forever being separated from her breaks my heart. I don't think I could stand not knowing how she's doing, or if she's happy or sad. I cannot think of a better way to further enrich our lives than having Kimmy share it with us. It'll be our first priority once we're back home in the states."

"I don't know what to say."

"No words needed, my love." Maggie eyed the bed. "Actions speak louder than words, anyway. Right?"

"They do."

"Then show me."

****

Hours later, languishing in love's afterglow, Maggie lay watching Claire dress.

"Are you sure you have to leave so soon?" Maggie asked.

"I do. Remember our agreement?"

"Yeah. Yeah. No sleepovers in the officers' building."

"Yes. It's too risky."

"All this sneaking around is damn annoying."

Claire bent and tied her sneakers. "It's better than my having to schlep back to ARC under the cover of night. I have to say, Maggie, that whatever you told Bunsen to get her to let me sleep in MSU from now on worked like a charm."

"It was one phone call and, believe you me, I think Buns was relieved to get rid of you. And, you're not actually sleeping in MSU but in a tent, for God's sake."

"I'm sleeping with the children, which is where I'm needed."

Maggie sighed. "You're going to be one hell of a mother one day, Claire."

"That makes two of us."

Maggie's walkie-talkie crackled to life. She punched a pillow. "Damn. Is there ever a break?" She snagged the receiver and depressed the speak button. "Calder here. Over."

A gravelly voice sounded. "Sergeant Pitman, Captain." Claire knew Pitman was Maggie's direct report for the day because Salvatore was overworked, burned out, and given a two day R and R. "There's another fire to put out, Captain."

"I'll meet you at HQ. Over."

"Another all-nighter?" Claire asked.

"It looks like it. I didn't want to talk about it earlier, but things are heating up in the battlefield."

"I know. Word gets around. It's disheartening."

"I hate to say it, Claire, but I think we're going to lose. The North is no longer abiding by the cease fire pact and is attacking small, remote areas of the South. It's as if the Paris Peace Accords agreement never existed."

Claire hugged herself. "What can we do?"

"The only thing we can do. Brace for impact."

****

January, 1975

Beneath a dim flashlight beam, Claire sat cross-legged on her cot and began to write.

Dear Mom and Dad,

I'm sorry for the delay in writing, but much has been happening and I haven't had a free moment to write it all down until now.

Claire went on to write about how the Christmas concert was a huge success and that the children delighted in their presents.

I, too, received a special present from Mag—

"Damn," Claire whispered, scribbling out 'Mag.' "I hate that everything is so goddamned censored here." She continued writing:

—a special someone. The girl orphan, Kimmy, the one I've bonded with the most, has been experiencing night terrors. She so reminds me of me, in the months after you and dad brought me home, when I, too, suffered from post trauma and would crawl into cardboard boxes to hide whenever a car backfired or a helicopter flew too low. It's heart-wrenching to witness, but thankfully, she has no recollection of her nightmares and they do seem to be lessening in frequency. I hope it's a sign that she's coming to terms with her emotional burden and is ready to move on. I have to tell you, Mom and Dad, that we've become so close that she's begun calling me "Má." I'm crazy about her!

She was also a bit of a loner at first but is finally breaking out of her shell and socializing with the other orphans. And, speaking of the other orphans, their progress has been nothing short of amazing, especially in terms of their learning and communicating bilingually.

I'm taking as many pictures as the base will allow, and one friend has even let me use her bathroom as a makeshift darkroom.

Thank you, again, for the monthly "care" packages you've been sending my way. They so remind me of the world that is waiting for me back in Hobarth. Oh, by the way, I can't believe that you both decided to keep the Christmas tree up so we can open presents together whenever I get a leave of absence. With the ways things are going, though, it could be awhile before that happens. We may be dying Easter eggs and opening presents at the same time.

Claire stopped and grimaced. Here came the hard part:

And, of course, the base is abuzz with the upsetting news that the North Vietnamese have taken such a stronghold, that it's feared the South will surrender and Saigon will fall under communist rule sooner rather than later. Because of this very real threat, Tan Son Nhut is beginning dismantlement protocols and a gradual withdrawal of certain U.S. personnel. The ARC is one of the first groups scheduled to return home. I know that this news comes as an answer to your prayers that we will soon be reunited, but my heart aches to tell you that I am torn between returning to a world I've known since I was a young child, and remaining in a world I'm only beginning to fully know. I can't help thinking that once we leave, what happens to the South Vietnamese who have placed so much trust in us? Who our troops walked side by side in the battlefield with in their fight for peace? And, worse yet, what happens to the children? The orphans who have no homes? Who will take care of them? The thought of putting them into refugee camps makes me sick to my stomach.

It is for these reasons I've come to a decision that may come as a hardship to you both. I've thought long and hard about this decision, so there's no changing my mind. I'm convinced that I need to remain in Vietnam, to serve the people left to pick up the shattered pieces of their lives, certainly not abandon them in their time of greatest need. It just makes sense. I'm not sure how I will be able to serve, or if I'm even allowed to remain in Vietnam, but I have to give it a try. As always, I do hope you will understand and respect my wishes.

Love, Claire

Chapter Thirteen

Cong Hoa Hospital, Saigon – February, 1975

Claire tightened the sash on her disposable gown before slipping on a pair of nitrile gloves. She glanced about the messy operating room and grimaced before setting to work collecting bloody sheets and towels from the main operating area and shoving them into a laundry basket. She then moved on to wad up gore-saturated gauze and bandages for waste disposal. A wave of nausea settled upon her, making her gag. She had to get out of the room. It reeked of death. But first, she had to sanitize the surgical utensils and scrub down the counters.

Claire had learned in no time flat that working in a hospital setting would be physically challenging and emotionally wearing, yet, she embraced the opportunity and thanked her lucky stars for her good fortune. From the moment she heard that TSN's base was being dismantled and that all non-military personnel needed to leave the area and return to the states, she became hell-bent on remaining in-country. And Maggie wholeheartedly agreed that there was still work to be done, and that leaving Vietnam at this crucial point would feel too much like desertion. Maggie had promised her that she would find a way to stay, come hell or high water.

And find it, she did. Maggie learned that the Red Cross sponsored a program called the Service to Military Hospitals Initiative, which was based in Saigon, an area that had not yet fallen under enemy attack. Claire's transfer was immediate, and Maggie soon followed serving as chief liaison to high-ranking heads of staff at the U.S. Embassy, also based in Saigon. The best part of all was that they were able to take the children with them. Although living arrangements were separate, Maggie had made sure that all of TSN's orphans were housed in the closest refugee camp to where they worked.

Once her duties were completed, Claire washed up and clocked out. Now, awash in bright sunshine, Claire bobbed and weaved between snarled traffic and the bustle of pedestrians in the congested Saigon suburb. She glanced at her wristwatch. If she hurried, she might be able to see Kimmy for a few minutes before supper.

Since the refugee camp was close to the hospital, Claire would often visit Kimmy on her lunch breaks to share a friendly wave or blow air kisses. On the rare occasion when Kimmy wasn't involved in schooling, they'd indulge in a warm, inviting hug. As the orphans were held to a strict regimen that only allowed free time and extended visits with loved ones on weekends, Claire took what she could get, any chance she could get.

Claire jogged the remaining distance to the refugee camp. She grinned when she caught sight of Kimmy standing at the back of the line of children waiting to return inside for showers and mealtime. As had become habit, Claire always put her best face forward whenever she was around Kimmy. In Kimmy's world, Claire made damn sure she didn't feel the emotional strain of worrying about the continuous travesties of war and the fear of an impending North Vietnamese occupation.

"Kimmy!" Claire shouted.

Kimmy's head whipped toward the sound of Claire's voice. When she saw her, she gave Claire a megawatt smile that warmed her to the core. When Kimmy took a step out of line, Claire held her hands in front of her to stop her. "Stay put, kiddo. I don't want you to get into trouble."

Kimmy's face crumpled into a pout. "But I miss you."

"Maggie and I miss you, too. So very much. But tomorrow is Saturday. And you know what that means, right?"

Kimmy jumped up and down. "It's our fun day."

"Yes, and what a fun day we have in store for you."

"Tell me! Tell me!"

"And ruin the surprise? Not on your life, kiddo."

A bell clanged twice, signaling the children to face forward and wait for an aide to usher them inside.

Claire blew Kimmy a final kiss and said, "I'll be here

bright and early to get you. We'll start the day with a pan-cake breakfast. How's that sound?"

"Groovy!"

"Okay, So, until then be there or...?"

"Be square!" Kimmy shouted.

"That's my girl!"

Claire waited until Kimmy disappeared from view before walking the half mile to the Embassy. As had become their habit, Claire met Maggie in a small garden area on Embassy property.

Claire found her seated on a bench with her legs spread and holding her head in her hands between them. With an exaggerated groan, Claire plopped down beside her with her legs splayed out. Maggie glanced at her and said, "You look like shit, McCallum."

Claire smirked in spite of her exhaustion. "That's what I like about you, Calder. You don't sugarcoat a damn thing."

"Operating room horrors?"

Claire shuddered. "Amputations seemed to be the main course today. Some were from warfare, others from para-sitic infection. The smell was godawful. And we're totally over capacity and understaffed. Trying to maintain a sterile environment amidst the chaos is getting worse by the day."

"I can sympathize with you. You've seen the horrors first-hand while I've been spared the view but not the gory details. I lost count of how many POWs I spoke to today. Fifty? A hundred? Who the hell knows? Their recounts of imprisonment and torture were sickening, heart-wrenching, and vile. I haven't been able to eat anything all day. I don't think I'd be able to keep it down."

Claire nodded. "I heard one of the doctors saying that the refugee camps aren't fairing much better. Refugees are flooding in from Laos, Thailand, and Cambodia, seeking aid and a safe haven for themselves and their children."

"What a shit show."

"Indeed. And we have front row seats." Maggie turned to face Claire on the bench. "You know that the time is drawing near, right?"

Claire swallowed hard. "That we'll have to flee Sai-gon?"

Maggie stood and balled her hands into fists.

"I'm afraid so. And it has to be an immediate response. You and I need to put together a go kit."

"What's a go kit?"

"A bag that carries everything of true importance to you. It needs to be small and lightweight and carried on your person from sun up to sun down in the event we have to drop everything and run."

"That shouldn't be too difficult. I didn't come with much so I'm sure as hell not leaving with much."

****

March, 1975

Claire stood at the Embassy gate, tapping her foot and checking her watch for the umpteenth time. Late again, Margaret Anne Calder with an *e*. Would she ever eat a warm supper?

Maggie finally appeared and Claire's annoyance fizzled. Something was definitely up. She hadn't seen Maggie this hepped up in months.

Maggie hustled toward her. "I know. I know. I'm late, but for good reason."

"From the look on your face you look like the cat that swallowed the canary."

When they were a safe distance away from the Embassy and any passersby, Maggie leaned in and whispered, "I've got some top-secret news to share."

"When you say top secret, doesn't that mean that you shouldn't tell anyone about it?" Claire teased.

"You're going to want to hear this. I heard from the top brass that President Ford's directed monies from a special foreign aid children's fund be made available to fly refugee children out of Saigon to the United States."

"For real?"

"It's totally on the up and up. The brass believes that if the children remain in country, their lives are in grave danger from communist military offenses."

"How many children are we talking?'

"Thousands. As we speak, an operating procedure and flight schedule is being devised for a mission called Operation Baby Rescue, which will be overseen by Military Aircraft Command. Tan Son Nhut is the centralized meet-up point for any refugee children who have migrated from neighboring areas."

"Wow, this is so unbelievable. What a huge undertaking. What can I do to help?"

"Come along for the ride."

Claire blinked. "What?"

Maggie gripped her by the shoulders so that they were eye to eye.

"As head of Medical Services, I'm in charge of overseeing the mission. And I want you and Kimmy, of course, to join me on Operation Baby Rescue's virgin flight to the U.S. We're going home, Claire."

"I...I...I..."

Maggie laughed. "I know, the news hit me like a freight train, too."

"Where are we going?"

"San Francisco. There's a huge army reserve center based in the Presidio area. One of its buildings, Harmon Hall, is being converted into a massive-care facility."

"Do you know when?"

"No, but I'm keeping my ear close to the ground. It has to happen before the wet season. April's the ideal month."

"I need to get word to my parents."

"No way."

"Only to let them know that I'll be coming home soon. And to set a few more plates at the dinner table." Claire pleaded with her eyes.

Maggie scratched her chin. "Hm. I know that any verbal contact via MARS is off limits, but maybe I could get someone in Communications to send out a telegram to your folks and have it delivered by courier. That way we're not wasting any military personnel in delivering it."

Claire resisted the urge to hug her.

"You are amazing. My knight...no, lady in shining armor."

Maggie did a mock bow. "Always at your service."

Chapter Fourteen

April, 1975

Maggie found Claire reviewing patient charts in Cong Hoa's admission area.

"Hey," Maggie said.

Claire beamed. "Hi. It's a little early for lunch. We're so busy, I doubt I'm going to take one today, anyway."

"It's happening, Claire. It's happening right now."

Claire slid the patient chart into a file bin. "What, exactly, is happening?

"Operation Baby Rescue is ready to take off."

It took a few seconds for Maggie's announcement to register. When it did, Claire's knees started to shake. "How... How much time do we have?"

"Not near enough. As we speak, a convoy of military buses has arrived in Saigon to transport the children to Tan Son Nhut. OBR's first official flight takes off this afternoon, at four. That's less than six hours from now. Your go-bag's ready, right? Packed with everything you'll need for a few days?"

"Yes. I keep it with me at all times. Yours?"

"In the escort Jeep waiting for us outside."

"Kimmy?"

"Already on the first bus to depart. You can meet up with her at Tan Son Nhut." Maggie checked her watch. "Engine's running, Claire. We have to leave. Now."

Claire grabbed her bag. "You go first. I'm right behind you."

****

When they arrived at Tan Son Nhut, Claire felt a strong sense of déjà vu. She looked wide-eyed at Maggie. "I can't believe it's been six months since I first stepped foot on this airstrip. It seems like an eternity."

Claire glanced around. "So familiar and yet so different. So stark. So devoid of activity. A ghost town."

"Yes, all but a few temporary tent shelters and their encampment areas remain. Most of the munitions hangars are cleared, as well as food provision storage. For the most part, Jeeps are gone, but you can find a few bikes lying around. As far as personnel, it's mostly skeleton crews that rotate every few days."

Tears welled in Claire's eyes. "This place is such a brutal reminder."

"Of what?"

"Of a war hard fought and hard lost."

Maggie gripped Claire's elbow. "Come. I have something to show you." Side by side, Maggie guided her past empty hangars and stacked wooden pallets. They turned a corner and Claire stopped short and gawked at the huge aircraft that loomed before her. Its immensity blocked out the sun.

"My God!"

"Meet Goliath," Maggie said. "This baby is going to fly us to freedom."

Claire whistled. "It's monstrous."

"Indeed. It's a Lockheed C-5A heavy lift transport. It's one mother of an airplane. Granted, it doesn't have the comforts of a commercial plane, and it's going to be a rough ride, but it's going to get all of us home."

Activity to her left caught Claire's attention. Standing beneath two huge canopies were hundreds of child refugees of varied ages being tended to by medical and service personnel. To her astonishment, many of the children were infants and toddlers that were either held or cradled on laps, or chased after by doting overseers. Claire felt a pang of unease. "Where are the older children? Kimmy?"

Maggie scoped the area. "Oh, there she is. She's playing hopscotch with the others." Maggie called out to Kimmy. When Kimmy looked up, she gave them an endearing smile and a wave.

"Okay, I'm ready. What's my assignment?"

Maggie tugged on Claire's camera strap. "For now, do

what you do best. Capture this momentous occasion on film."

"But this is supposed to be a top secret mission."

"Trust me when I say that no enemy will ever set eyes on your pics, but the American public will. This is your chance, Claire. Go for it."

Claire arched a brow. "Better late than never, right?"

"You got it, baby."

"Captain Calder! Claire!"

They turned and saw Salvatore bustling toward them. He saluted Maggie. "Food and water provisions, as well as baby essentials are being loaded first. Once that's taken care of, we can start the boarding process."

"Excellent." Maggie turned to Claire. "That's when you're going to be needed the most, to help service personnel with getting all of these little bundles of joy on Goliath."

"Do you have any idea where Kimmy and I will be seated?"

"Together in the cargo area."

Claire felt the weight of a bowling ball settle in her gut. "Cargo area?"

Salvatore looked back and forth between the two before making a hasty retreat.

Maggie nodded. "Goliath is equipped with two decks. The lower deck, known as the cargo area, runs the entire plane length. The older kids and adults will either be strapped to the cargo deck or occupy two aluminum benches on either side of the main cargo area. The infants, which make up the bulk of OBR's passengers, will be secured two to a seat on the upper deck."

Claire gnawed at her bottom lip. "We'll be strapped down?"

"Don't worry. We'll do our best to make sure that everyone is comfortable and safe. It's the only way. And..."

"Spit it out, Calder."

"I hate to break this to you, but only medical personnel and officers are permitted on Goliath's upper deck, in the troop compartment area, during the flight."

Claire tried to make light of her disappointment. "No first-class accommodations for lovers, huh?"

"I'm afraid not. I promise you that once we reach the States, I'll be first in line to welcome you and Kimmy on home turf."

"I'm going to hold you to that promise."

Maggie lowered her voice. "I wish I could kiss you right here, right on this blasted tarmac in front of the entire US Military."

"As we know that's not going to happen this close to freedom, I guess I'm going to have to settle for an 'I love you, Claire' and a promise of wild, passionate love in the very near future."

"I love you, Claire."

Claire's heart soared with happiness. "How much?"

"More than mere words could ever express." Maggie tapped her watch. "I have to go. Duty calls."

"Where?"

"I'm overseeing ground support in fueling and preflight inspections. Most likely, this will be the last time we'll see each other before takeoff."

Claire forced a smile. "Well, on the bright side, at least I'll be sharing space with Kimmy."

Maggie poked Claire's camera. "Get busy, woman. This flight's going to be chronicled in the history books, and I want you to have first dibs on the photo rights."

Claire grinned and set off in search of the perfect shot. This time, though, as she aimed, focused, and snapped, she didn't feel much emotional gratification. It was as if everyone on the base had a specific duty, an important one to attend to, whereas she felt like picture taking might be a way of passing time and not amount to anything meaningful. On this day, she wanted to be hands' on, not a casual observer. On this day, the world was going to change and her life with it. She wanted to be active and take in the whole scene instead of seeing it through a small, circular lens.

At one point, she stopped to observe a group of servicewomen lining two-foot-square cardboard storage boxes with thin layers of fabric foam. A shudder raced up her spine. Must be infant transports. To Claire, they looked like miniature caskets. She shook her head to clear the morbid thought.

Within a half hour, a bugle sounded, followed by a speaker announcement. "All systems are go. Boarding process can commence."

Claire backtracked to where Kimmy had been playing. Already, service personnel were gathering the children into groups of five.

Claire sidled up to a red-haired woman in gray fatigues. "I'm Claire McCallum. ARC. I'm here to help with the children."

The woman wiped a damp handkerchief across her sweaty brow. "Thank the heavens. We can use all the help we can get. As you can see, the children are separated into groups. Each group will be supervised by one adult. So, feel free to take your pick of what group you want to be responsible for looking after during the flight."

"Thank you."

Claire hurried to where Kimmy stood with two boys and two girls Claire recognized from the refugee camp. "So, gang, are you all ready for the adventure of your life?"

"Are we going to Africa?" the boy asked.

"Not on this trip."

"You're silly, Quan," the girl said. "We're going to the United States of America. It is the land of the free and the home of the brave, right? That's what Ms. Worth told us at the camp."

Claire squeezed the girl's shoulder. She remembered a conversation she'd once had with Quincy where Quincy had voiced her disillusionment of the U.S. when it came to overcoming social barriers. Although Claire couldn't disagree, she remained optimistic that change for the better should never be a lost cause. "Then the US is as good a fresh start as any other place."

Claire glanced at Kimmy, saw the panicked expression on her face. "What's wrong, kiddo?"

Kimmy lips trembled. "It's too big. It won't fly. We will fall from the sky."

Trepidation prickled Claire's skin and she wondered if Kimmy was picking up on her own anxiety about the flight. Claire knelt beside her and forced a smile. "I promise you, Kimmy, that the plane is safe. That we will be safe."

Kimmy blinked back tears. "You promise?"

"Yes. I promise."

Claire thought of an idea to take Kimmy's mind off the impending flight.

She unslung her satchel from around her neck, double-knotted its strap to shorten its length, and slid it over Kimmy's head. The satchel was so big, it covered most of Kimmy's chest. In an instant, the tears were gone and Kimmy was running her fingers over the colorful fabric patches.

"Will you keep this safe for me while I help the others onto the plane?"

Kimmy's face lit up like a Fourth of July firework celebration. "Oh yes, Má. Yes, I will!"

"Good. Now, it's time to get on board. Is everybody ready?"

All five of her charges shouted in unison, "Yes!"

Claire snagged a small brown bag off a service cart. "Okay, but before we go, I want each of you to put these small wads of wax in your ears. The plane can get mighty noisy, and we don't want your ears to hurt."

* * * *

Upon takeoff, Claire closed her eyes, gritted her teeth, and held fast to the tie-down straps that secured her in a sitting position in the cargo hold. Kimmy sat, restrained, on an aluminum bench within arm's reach. As Goliath gained altitude at an accelerated rate of speed, Claire cupped her ears over the deafening roar of its dual engines and prayed.

Goliath rose ever higher, defying the forces of gravity, and a cacophony of metallic sounds drowned out the whimpers and wails coming from its young passengers. All the while during Goliath's ascent, Claire tried to focus on positive thoughts. Soon, she, Maggie, and Kimmy would be back home. Soon, a new day would dawn on them with the promise of a new life they would share—

Boom! Something exploded, sending a shockwave through the plane.

Kimmy let out a shriek of terror and clawed at Claire's

arm. Claire winced. Over the barrage of noise, Claire shouted, "It's okay, Kimmy. It's okay. Hold on to my hand." Within seconds, the compartment filled with thick, noxious smoke. All Claire could make out were ghostly shadows. Claire looked to her left and screamed. The explosion ripped a huge hole in Goliath's tail section. Depressurized air sucked equipment and items not battened down through the yawning gap. Horrified, Claire watched as children were torn from their restraints and flung about the cargo hold like ragdolls. Watched as adults risked their own safety by releasing their restraints and throwing themselves atop their tiny bodies to keep them from being sucked out the gaping abyss.

The plane violently bucked upward before slamming down into an air pocket that rattled her brain with pain. The intensity of the motion made her lose her grip on Kimmy's hand. In a panic, Claire felt around in the darkness for her. There was nothing but air. She shouted Kimmy's name over and over. No response. Claire tasted something warm and metallic in her mouth. Blood. She'd bit her tongue. Every fiber of her being urged her to move into rescue mode, but her limbs refused to respond. They were paralyzed by fear.

Another explosion blasted within the compartment. In reaction, Goliath shuddered and began to nosedive. Cries of terror, panic, and pain echoed in Claire's ears. Through sheer willpower, she broke through her paralysis and untied her retraining straps. She lunged across the cargo hold to assist a nurse in stabilizing a boy gushing blood from a head wound. When Claire looked into the nurse's eyes, she saw dread. Everyone was going to die.

As Goliath lost altitude, it banked from side to side. Claire heard the mind-grating sound of shredding metal and an ear-splitting noise that sounded like a runaway train going off the rails. Then, impact. And then, nothingness.

****

Claire lay on her stomach atop a patch of charred grass. Through a thick haze of black smoke, she looked upon a scene right out of a war movie. All of her inherent senses were heightened. Her eyes teared from the acrid smoke. She smelled the stench of burning fuel and rubber. She heard the anguished wails and felt the grit of broken glass and sharp metal slivers beneath her fingertips. And she saw adults and children scattered across the debris-strewn landscape as far as she could see. Their bodies were contorted in a way that indicated broken bones. And there was blood. Lots of it. And body parts. And...

Claire closed her eyes and tried to block out the gruesome images. Again, her mind urged her body to move, but no muscles responded. She tried to speak, but all that came out were gurgling sounds. She knew she must be injured, but her body felt numb and cold, immune to pain. This nightmare world she'd been thrust into swirled out of control, and swam in and out of focus until, finally, she passed out.

Chapter Fifteen

Claire woke from a deep slumber, groggy and disoriented. She wrinkled her nose at the pungent smell of rubbing alcohol and bleach. Through a hazy white film, she took in her surroundings and tried to focus on details. Everything looked white. Pure white. She lifted her head a fraction of an inch and looked down. Okay, she was in a bed, and a bunch of tubes and wires were stuck to her body and hooked up to that damn noisy machine. The room echoed with its incessant hums, blips, and beeps. Claire had to be in a hospital. But what the hell for?

The past came rushing back with such intensity that Claire cried out and clamped her eyelids shut. A split second later, she heard the patter of footsteps and felt a whoosh of displaced air as someone came to her side and placed warm hands upon hers. When she managed to open her eyelids to slits, she looked up at her mother's tear-stained face. Her stomach tightened into a knot, and with a haggard breath, she broke down. Claire kept blinking to keep her mother's face in focus, but the tears kept coming and Sherri remained a blurred image. *She's here. Mom's here. She'll make everything better.*

"Mom," Claire rasped. Her throat felt as if razor blades were grating against her skin.

"Oh, Claire," Sherrie exclaimed, showering her with kisses. "Thank all the saints in heaven you've regained consciousness. That you've come back to us."

"Did I make it home?"

"No, dear. You're in a Saigon trauma hospital. The extent of your injuries prevented you from travel. Your dad and I flew out as soon as we learned of the accident."

Claire strained to speak. "Did anyone make it out alive?"

"Shh, Claire. You need to rest. We can talk later. Let me get the nurse."

Claire held fast to her mother's hand, preventing her from moving. "I need to know what happened, Mom. Now, not later."

Her mother's lower lip quivered. "There was a mechanical issue with the plane. The flight crew tried to stabilize the plane for an emergency return to Tan Son Nhut, but all systems failed and they were forced to make a crash landing in a rice paddy. When the plane hit the ground, it broke into pieces. The military's conducting a formal investigation. It may take months before they release their findings."

Claire swallowed hard. "Casualties, Mom? How many?"

"Claire, maybe it's not the right time to discuss—"

"How many, Mom?"

Sherri sighed and gripped Claire's hand tighter. "Officials estimate that close to half the passengers on board Goliath perished. That includes children, flight personnel, and medical and humanitarian aides. Search and rescue are still working at the scene, trying to find victims."

"What do you mean find?"

Sherri's voice trembled. "Search crews haven't been able to identify some bodies."

Claire recoiled in horror. Half of Goliath's passengers were dead? Claire remembered Maggie saying that close to three hundred people were on board. *Oh, my sweet Jesus...Maggie...Kimmy.*

"It's a miracle anyone survived," Claire heard her mother say from within a dense fog.

Oh Maggie, are you dead? And Kimmy, dear sweet Kimmy, could you be dead, too?

Claire voiced her worst fear. "Have the officials released a list of the—" She choked. "The dead?"

"I don't think so, Claire."

Claire pulled free of her mother's grip and tried to sit up. When she did, a violent bout of vertigo sent the rooming spinning. Thunderbolts of pain seared her skull. With an anguished moan, Claire collapsed backward onto the mattress.

Claire heard her mother's alarmed voice calling to her from a distance, but the pain was so all-consuming that she couldn't respond. Mercifully, she lost consciousness.

****

When Claire again awoke, her mother and father stood like sentinels at her bedside while a staff nurse pressed the cool metallic end of a stethoscope against her chest.

"Heart rate's stable, and oxygen and blood levels are within normal range. You're one lucky woman, Ms. McCallum," the nurse said.

Claire remembered the crash, and the small bodies being flung about the cargo hold. Such young, innocent victims whose lives were so violently cut short. She would've gladly traded her life if it meant that at least one child could've survived. "How come I don't feel lucky?" Claire snapped.

The nurse opened her mouth to say something, must've thought better of it, and left.

Claire's father cleared his voice. "Your surgeon informed us that you may be able to come home soon. He's ordered another series of brain scans..."

Claire gripped her father by the wrist and squeezed hard. "Wait. Did I hear you right, Dad? Did you say brain scans?"

Mike covered Claire's hand until her grip loosened. "Yes. You suffered severe head trauma, a few fractured ribs, and numerous lacerations and contusions. You've undergone two surgeries to reduce brain swelling and control brain bleeds. You lapsed into a coma—"

Claire's mind reeled and, for a moment, she couldn't breathe. "Coma?" She gasped. "Dad, you're not making sense."

"You've been in a coma for two weeks, Claire. It was touch and go for a while if you'd ever regain consciousness—"

"But that's all in the past," Sherri hurriedly said. "You're now well on the road to recovery."

Claire felt as if she'd been punched in the gut. "You mean to tell me that I've been out for two weeks? That it's been two weeks since the crash?"

Mike nodded.

Claire again struggled to sit up and was struck by a tidal wave of pain that made her screech and clutch the sides of her head.

"You need to rest," Mike said, pressing against her shoulders.

"No! I need to get out of here. I need to find Maggie. And Kimmy. I can't waste any more time."

"Claire, upsetting yourself is only going to make your hospital stay longer."

"I'm getting the nurse," Sherri said.

Seconds later, the nurse appeared with a loaded syringe at the ready.

"No! No! No!" Claire screamed. "Why won't any of you listen to me? There's no time to spare!"

"There, there," the nurse said, before sticking a needle into a port in Claire's arm.

And the world around Claire turned from color, to gray, to black.

Chapter Sixteen

May, 1975 - McCallum House – Six Weeks Post-Crash

Claire thought that after finally being released from the hospital to continue recuperation at home, she'd be ecstatic. Nothing seemed farther than the truth. Most of the time, she felt as if she were walking through a dense fog. Sleep was sporadic and more nightmare-ridden than peaceful. She cried a lot. Gut-wrenching sobs that tore at her core and scared the livings daylights out of her mother. And she was tired all the time. So goddamn tired. She could barely make it to lunchtime without having to take a nap. Her loss of appetite made her weak, lethargic. All she kept thinking was that she was never going to get better. That she would never be able to find out what happened to Maggie and Kimmy. She thought she was losing her mind.

Sherri McCallum called from the second floor landing. "Claire? Claire? Are you awake?"

Awoken from a light doze, Claire grumbled, "I am now."

"Oh, good. You have a phone call, dear."

Claire glanced at the clunky, black rotary telephone perched on her side table. Funny. She hadn't heard it ring. Her mom probably turned off the sound. "Who is it?"

"A woman named Beatrice."

Claire bolted forward in her bed and immediately regretted the sudden movement. A fresh wave of pain seared across her chest, making her double over. Damn fractured ribs. Will they ever heal? With her heart pounding like a bass drum, she brought the receiver to her ear. "Beatrice. Thank God."

"Claire. Oh, Claire, it's been so long."

"I've been trying to reach you for weeks."

"I just returned to base from a reconnaissance mission overseas. I got your messages. What's up?"

"I wanted to know if you'd help me try to find Maggie."

A long stretch of silence echoed from the other end of the line.

"Beatrice? Hello, Beatrice? Are you there?"

Beatrice answered in a low, somber voice. "Yes, Claire. I'm here." She'd changed. Any trace of Beatrice's once out-spoken, boisterous personality was gone.

"Oh. Phew. For a minute there, I thought the call dropped. As I was saying—"

"Maggie's not missing, Claire."

Claire's felt a flicker of hope ignite deep within her heart. "Do you mean she's been found? That she's alive?"

"Maggie's dead. There's nothing more to do."

"No. That's not true. There hasn't been a clear determination."

"Claire, when the plane crashed, close to half of the bodies were burned beyond recognition. Some were children, but many were adults."

"But the passenger manifest…"

"The manifest has not been recovered, which leaves us with no definitive list of who was on board Goliath that day."

"But—"

"Don't you think if Maggie had survived, she would've reached out to us by now?"

"Maybe she can't. Maybe she's in a coma. Maybe—"

"No, Claire. Maggie's dead. I'm grieving her loss and trying to move on. Some days it's easier to cope than others. We all need to make peace. Maggie would've wanted that."

Claire gripped the phone so tight that her knuckles turned white. "I can't believe that, Beatrice. I won't believe that."

"Denial isn't healthy, Claire."

"It's not denial. It's a strong feeling, a sense, that Maggie is alive."

For the second time during their conversation, Claire's words were met with silence. Unable to accept the possibility that all hope was lost, Claire hung up the receiver and wept.

****

Days after her phone conversation with Beatrice, Claire couldn't bring herself to accept the fact that Maggie and Kimmy may be dead. What would be the point to her life if that were true? What about her hopes and dreams? Of living happily ever after? Was it all just a sick joke? A fabrication?

She'd started the day off with the intent to write to everyone she knew for help in locating Maggie and Kimmy. She'd made it to mid-afternoon before a profound feeling of hopelessness overcame her and she crawled into bed and muffled her sobs in her pillow. God, what was she going to do?

There was a sharp knock on the bedroom door. Shit. Why couldn't everyone just leave her alone? If she wanted to wallow in her despair, so be it. She didn't need the forced pep talks, or the constant questions as to how she'd slept, or are the nightmares gone, and all that other happy horseshit. She needed to come to terms with her loss in her own due time. As had become habit, Claire caressed the ruby pendant Maggie had given her as an engagement present. In some small way, it calmed her.

The raps on the door multiplied and became more insistent. "Claire? Claire, dear, are you all right?"

Claire swiped at her eyes and sniffled. "I've been better, Mom."

"Can I come in?"

The door opened before Claire responded.

Sherri swept the room in a glance and saw the stack of letters piling up on Claire's desk. "It's good to see that you've been hard at work. I better send Dad out to get more stamps."

Claire blew her nose. "Oh, what's the use?" she asked. "I feel like all I'm doing is going through the motions."

Sherri sat beside her. "That's where you're wrong."

"But Mom, it's been weeks since I sent letters to all of Maggie's superior officers and service members under her command with no word back. I even sent one to Sergeant

Salvatore, her top aide, and haven't heard anything, which makes me scared to death to think that he died in the crash with the others." Claire threw up her hands. "It's just so awful!"

"You said so yourself that after the Fall of Saigon, military personnel were transferred to so many different locations, it'd make your head spin. That letters need to go through military channels and then filtered out from there. I imagine it's a daunting process."

"But, don't you think they should know something by now? It's been close to two months since the crash."

"Claire, I fear your search has only begun and that you must be patient and not lose heart."

"It's hard not to, Mom. And Maggie is only one piece of the puzzle. There's Kimmy, too. There's a bunch of refugee processing centers on the west coast, but I can't travel until I get medical clearance from old Doc Woodruff, which could be weeks. And all of those pictures I took at Tan Son Nhut..." Claire's voice hitched. "Destroyed in the crash. All I have is a description and an approximate age, which isn't much considering numerous other OBR flights have departed from Saigon since the crash and landed safely stateside. I've read in the paper that there are now thousands of displaced children being cared for at these centers."

Sherri jumped to her feet.

"What?" Claire asked.

"Pictures," Sherri said. "You said you lost all of the pictures in the crash."

"Yes."

"Maybe not."

"Huh?"

"Give me a sec. I'll be right back."

Claire shook her head. Sometimes parents could be so weird.

The sound of rummaging echoed down the hall, followed by hurried footsteps. Sherri returned holding a thin envelope with Fotomat's printed logo on its front flap.

"I knew it. In the weeks before you decided to develop your film on base, you sent a few rolls home for developing. I have them right here. Maybe we'll get lucky and Kimmy will be in one of them."

Claire gasped. "For real? I totally forgot about them."

"Your Dad and I put them away for safe keeping while you recuperated. We thought showing them to you before you were ready would depress you even more."

Claire retrieved the envelope from Sherri's hands and undid the flap. Her fingers trembled when she slid the photos onto the bedspread. Second picture in, Claire brought a fist to her lips to stifle a gasp.

"There you are, my lovely child," Claire whispered. "There you are."

The picture was a wide-angle view of Kimmy and a few orphans folding origami shapes at an activity table. A few other photos were action shots of Kimmy and the orphans at play.

"Which one is Kimmy?" Sherri asked.

Claire pointed. "There, wearing the yellow sundress."

"My, she's darling. All of them are. And Maggie?"

Claire scanned the rest of the photos. For a moment, she stopped breathing. Maggie was in one photo, standing off to the far right. Her head was tilted to the side, and she was smiling.

"Th...th... There."

Sherri studied the picture. "She's beautiful."

Claire blinked back tears. "She's the love of my life."

"I know, Claire."

Claire stared at her. "You do?"

Sherri squeezed Claire's hands. "I do. The way you gushed on about her in your letters told me all I needed to know."

This time, when the tears streamed down her cheeks, Claire made no move to wipe them away. "We were going to have a life together here. And adopt Kimmy. We were going to be a fa...fa...family."

Sherri opened her arms. "Oh, dear Claire. Come here." Claire fell into her embrace and surrendered to uncontrollable sobs. Without a word, Sherri lulled Claire until her tears subsided and she regained a semblance of composure.

"And then there's the guilt, Mom. It's eating me up inside."

Sherri pulled away. "Guilt? Over loving a woman? That's silly. It's who you are."

"No. Not about being gay. My guilt is that I survived the crash when maybe Maggie and Kimmy, and all of those innocent children, didn't. I mean, I told Kimmy that the plane was safe. I lied to her."

Sherri gripped Claire's shoulders. "Claire Hien McCallum. I'll say this once, so you better listen."

Claire knew that whenever her mother used her full name, including her Vietnamese surname, she meant business and that it'd be wise for Claire to keep her mouth shut.

Sherri continued. "What you're suffering from is survivor's guilt. The 'why couldn't it have been me' guilt. This type of thinking is common after experiencing trauma, but it's displaced. You were meant to survive to serve a purpose in this life. It's not your time. You must honor the people you have loved and lost by moving on. If not, their deaths were in vain. Do you understand me?"

"I do, Mom. It's just so hard."

"What's hard is picking up where you left off."

Sherri nodded toward the desk. "Who else have you written to?"

"My ARC buddies and other friends I've made during my stay at TSN. There's one—his name's George—who I haven't been able to locate yet."

"You will, dear. As for the others, I'll make sure they're in the evening mail."

Claire reached for the picture of Kimmy. "Mom, do you think Dad could take the negative to this picture down to Fotomat and have Kimmy's image enlarged? And then make a bunch of copies? I'm going to need them when I visit the processing centers."

"Claire, I'm so excited, I can't wait for your Dad to get home from work to do the run. I'm going to do it myself. And I'm going to have them make hundreds of prints. Hundreds, I tell you."

"Oh, Mom. I don't know how to say thank you."

Sherri beamed at her. "You just did, my dear. You just did."

Chapter Seventeen

June, 1975

Sherri barged into Claire's bedroom with a smile so wide, whatever snide remark Claire wanted to say to her for entering her ultra-private domain without knocking was forgotten. "Claire, I'm beside myself with excitement."

"I can see that. Anything I should know about?"

Sherri made a beeline to where Claire sat at her desk and hugged her like a sumo wrestler.

"Geez, Mom," Claire grumbled, breaking free of her grasp, "you know I hate overdramatic shows of affection."

Sherri laughed. "Time to change your ways, Claire. What with it being the seventies and with free love being all the rage."

Claire didn't have the heart to tell her that free love meant freedom to pursue sex with whomever one pleased. "Whatever, Mom. What is this great news you have to share?"

"Doc Woodruff just called. He's reviewed your progress reports and most recent brain scans and has signed your release from medical care as of today. You're free, Claire. Home free. You've got your life back."

Claire bolted up from the desk and gripped Sherri's hands. "You mean it?"

"I do."

"Then I better start packing."

"And I better get your suitcase out of the attic. You've got a granddaughter to bring home to us."

****

Now given the all clear to travel, Claire booked the first nonstop, commercial flight from New York to San Francisco and landed there the next day, early-afternoon. She wasted no time hailing a cab and directing the driver to take her to the Presidio.

The cab dropped her at the reserve center, and Claire made several inquiries until she found herself standing at the Operation New Arrivals desk at Harmon Hall. When the receptionist noticed her, Claire said, "Good morning. My name is Claire McCallum. I served with the American Red Cross in Vietnam. I'm here to see a Ms. Sasha Mendez."

The receptionist smiled and handed Claire a clipboard and pen. "Please have a seat over there, and fill out this admittance form."

Claire sat and scanned the form. Not much to it, really. Its completion should have taken her less than two minutes. Should have, but one question stood out in big, bold letters, glaring at her from the page: Purpose of Visit. Claire twirled the pen in her fingers. Should she lie? Should she say she was a mother in search of her lost daughter? It sure as hell would cut through a lot of red tape if she claimed Kimmy's birth records were destroyed in the crash. After all, Kimmy had already gotten into the habit of calling her *Má,* anyway. And no one would question their ethnicity. It'd really be quite easy. But then Claire remembered her mother telling her that lies always led to more lies and no good ever came of them.

"Ms. McCallum?"

Claire looked up to see a tall woman with flawless, light-brown skin, a cropped black afro, and eyes the color of amber standing before her. The woman extended her hand. "Hi. My name is Sasha Mendez. I'm a liaison with the Peace Corps. I'm your escort for today's visit."

Claire returned the smile and handshake. "I'm pleased to meet you, Ms. Mendez."

"Oh, please, call me Sasha. No formalities here."

"Sasha, then."

"I've been told that you're interested in visiting our child refuge housing area."

"Yes."

"With the hope to…?"

Claire decided honesty was the way to go. "Adopt one of the children."

"Do you have a preference?"

"Preference?"

Sasha giggled. "Yes, are you looking for a boy? Or a girl?"

"Oh, sorry. A girl."

Sasha whipped out a spiral-bound notepad and began writing. "Any specific age?"

"Kimmy would be close to five or six by now."

Sasha stopped writing and looked at Claire. "Kimmy?"

Claire nodded.

"You have a specific child in mind?"

"I do. I even have a picture of her to help narrow down the search." Claire reached inside her overnight bag and handed Sasha an eight-by-ten glossy of Kimmy.

"Claire, if you don't mind my asking... How do you know Kimmy?"

"She was orphaned. I cared for her while at Tan Son Nhut. We were both on the first OBR flight out of Saigon."

Sasha blanched. "You mean the one that crashed?"

Claire nodded.

"Dear Lord, such a horrific event. It's a miracle anyone survived. You deserve a medal of honor for bravery."

Claire experienced a sudden flashback of the moments before the crash, when she was so consumed by terror that she couldn't move to help any of the children. She didn't deserve any damn medal. She gave Sasha a small, polite smile. "It's my hope that Kimmy is also a survivor, and I intend to find her and provide her with a stable, loving home."

"Rest assured, I'll do everything in my power to assist in your search. What is Kimmy's last name?

"Nguyen."

Sasha frowned. "Nguyen's a common Vietnamese name."

Claire's chest tightened. "I know this isn't going to be easy, but I have to start somewhere."

"Understood. First things first. Together, we'll check out the children residing here, at Harmon Hall. Some of them were survivors of the crash and sent here to recuperate after being hospitalized for their injuries. Since then, though, thousands of more refugees have arrived, so it won't be a simple pick-one-out-of-a-lineup deal. There are also many refugees who, due to severe injury, have remained hospitalized in locations throughout the Bay area. We can check them out if we don't find Kimmy here."

"How many hospitals are we talking about?"

"Maybe fifteen or so."

Claire bit her tongue to stop herself from screaming.

Sasha continued with a rundown of the search process, seemingly unaware of Claire's mounting frustration. "Shall we get started?" she eventually asked.

Harmon Hall was massive and segregated from any base operations. It reminded Claire of a handful of school gymnasiums grouped into one. It consisted of large areas partitioned off by curtains along its perimeter.

"Each partitioned area serves a specific function such as records management, adoption prep and review, et cetera, et cetera.' Sasha said. "Another section oversees basic needs such as providing clothing, food, and as-needed medical treatment."

"This is amazing. Who oversees operations here?"

"U.S. Army Forces Command, but they're far from the only ones. We have ARC volunteers like yourself, former veterans, civic communities, and a list as long as my arm of humanitarian organizations all lending a helping hand. Not to mention a huge outpouring of donations from the American people. Hands down, Operation Baby Rescue's truly an unprecedented endeavor. And, keep in mind that HH isn't the only processing center on the west coast so if you strike out here, there are other options."

"Operations seem so…fluid."

"In the beginning, when we were at a maxed-out capacity, it was a nightmare trying to keep the refugees clean, fed, and medicated. Now that other processing centers are active, our managed care system has greatly improved. The children here are healthy. Heck, many have already been adopted."

Claire stopped short. Her voice rose a few pitches higher than normal. "Wait. Many have been adopted? So soon?"

Sasha's smile wavered. "Please forgive me. It must feel

like yesterday to you. In reality, it's been close to three months since OBR was initiated."

Of course it had been three months, most of which she'd spent either in a coma, recuperating from surgery, or emotionally unable to function. Damn, she wished it hadn't taken her so long to get her shit together.

Sasha must have picked up on Claire's despair because she quickly added, "We do have age on our side."

"Age?"

"Yes. What we've been noticing is that a high percentage of adoptees are infants or toddlers. Sad to say, only a small portion of older orphans have been placed in adoptive homes."

"Are most of the older children housed here?"

"A few have been placed in temporary foster homes to offset the crowding issue. I can check the records. Claire..."

Claire touched Sasha's arm. "Please, speak your mind. No question is off limits."

"Are you certain that Kimmy survived the crash, when so many on board Goliath perished?"

"I don't know anything for certain, but I can't stop looking for her until I know the truth."

Sasha smiled. "Kimmy is lucky to have you on her side."

"I'm the lucky one to have her in my life."

Sasha patted Claire's shoulder. "Well, as you can see, we've arrived at the infant ward. Why don't you hang out here while I get a refugee print out?"

"Will do."

Tears welled in Claire's eyes as she watched volunteers and trained personnel tend to the infants and toddlers. Refugee babies were lined up, lengthwise, three to a mattress. Volunteers filled plastic basins with warm water and placed the basins, washcloths, and towels beside each infant. A group of volunteers bathed and towel-dried the infants before handing them off to another group of volunteers to lotion, powder, diaper, and dress. Still another group stood at the ready to either bottle- or spoon-feed them.

Within moments, Sasha returned with a mimeographed copy.

"We're all set. I'm told that the older children are outside in the play area. The volunteers are switching them out for showers. From what I can gather, about thirty of them are survivors from the crash, twenty of which are girls."

Claire took a deep breath, mouthed a silent prayer to the powers that be, and followed in Sasha's footsteps. Once outside, she shaded her eyes from the sun's glare so she could focus on a large, fenced-in play area. Claire counted twenty groups of ten to fifteen children each. Each group was participating in some type of physical activity from calisthenics to competitive relay races, to games of tag or jump rope marathons. Claire's smiled at the sounds of laughter. The children's obvious enjoyment reminded her of her time on Tan Son Nhut, with her own small brood of orphans and Maggie by her side. Oh, Maggie. She missed her so damn much.

Sasha interrupted Claire's thoughts. "I suggest taking on one group at a time."

"Fine by me."

"Now remember. Try not to get discouraged if we don't find Kimmy on our first sweep. There are other centers. And don't forget the hospitals."

Claire bit her lip. "I'll try to remain optimistic."

"That's the spirit."

****

The extension rang four times before it was picked up.

"Hello? McCallum residence." Mom's cheery voice.

"Hi, Mom. It's me."

"Oh, thank God. Your father and I have been pacing the floors waiting to hear from you. And, of course, now that he stepped out to get milk and butter, you call and he misses it. Boy, he's going to be heated."

"It was the first chance I got, Mom. It's been a really chaotic day."

"How was the flight?"

"Bumpy."

"Any anxiety attacks?"

"A few, but I survived."

"Well, the important thing is that you arrived in one piece."

Claire winced. Sometimes Mom had a way of putting her foot in her mouth.

"So…any luck?"

"Harmon Hall was a bust, Mom."

"I'm so sorry, honey. But tomorrow's another day, right? Full of bright sunshine and promise."

Claire swallowed hard. "Yes. A woman from the Peace Corps is accompanying me to area hospitals that treated some of the injured children from the crash. I have to confess, though, that I don't hold out much hope of finding Kimmy there."

"Why not?"

Claire kneaded a knot of tension at the base of her neck. "I would think that after all these months, most of the injured kids would have recovered and been released to Harmon Hall, or the other two processing centers."

"Thinking and knowing are two different things, Claire."

"I know that, Mom."

"Remember what I said about not losing heart, okay?"

"Yes, Mom."

"And how about lodging?"

"Harmon Hall has that covered, too. They're putting me up in a private bunk area for the length of my stay."

"Oh, good. You must be famished."

"Not really."

"Now, Claire, you need to keep up your strength."

"Yes, Mom."

"Promise to call tomorrow? I'll make sure your dad stays put the whole day."

"Yes, Mom."

"In the meantime and, as the Dionne Warwick song goes, 'I'll say a little prayer for you.'"

"Thanks, Mom."

Later, Claire lay on a cot, thinking about her mother's words about not losing heart. Was this her fate? Was she doomed to be like Maggie, who wore a black heart around her neck to mourn her murdered lover? Who rejected everything good in life because the burden to be happy was too much to bear? Claire stroked the ruby pendant, but tonight it offered no comfort.

Chapter Eighteen

As agreed, Sasha met Claire outside the admissions department at 9:00 a.m. With a grin, Sasha handed Claire a Styrofoam cup of coffee and a bagel.

"I took it upon myself to add a few sugars and some creamer, if that's okay."

Claire took a sip and sighed. "Perfect."

"And I added cream cheese to the bagel, but not enough for it to get gooey and hard to handle."

"Thank you."

"Sure thing." She pointed to a beige sedan parked outside the gate. "That's our ride. Ready?"

Claire let out a nervous chuckle. "As ready as I'll ever be."

As they drove, Sasha filled Claire in on the latest news. "First thing this morning, I checked with the foster homes. None of the children are under ten years old."

"And the ones already adopted?"

"Still awaiting word. I then checked with the hospitals, and it appears our list of fifteen sites has been reduced to three still treating survivors from the crash."

"How many patients in total?"

"Eight females and seven males. We can exclude five from the eight females because they're in their early-to-mid teens, way older than Kimmy. The remaining three, all in different hospitals no less, are Jane Does, but they're in Kimmy's age range."

"Why are they Jane Does when they're old enough to know their own names?"

"Two are comatose, and one's on a ventilator."

Claire clutched her chest. "Sweet Jesus."

"I know. I can't imagine the pain these children have endured. I mapped out hospital locations and Children's Hospital is the farthest. I figure we can start there and work our way back."

****

Three grueling hours later, Sasha and Claire returned to Harmon Hall with heavy hearts and dashed hopes.

"Either the proverbial haystack's getting bigger, or the needle's getting smaller," Claire said. "I don't know what else to say, or what else to do. I feel like we've reached a dead end."

Sasha squeezed Claire's shoulder. "Hang tough, Claire. Your search has only begun."

Claire gritted her teeth so hard her jaw ached. "It's hard not to feel beaten. Maybe Kimmy is dead. Maybe I'm holding on to a false belief that she's alive and well."

"I distinctly remember you telling me that you won't stop searching for Kimmy until you know the truth."

"Maybe never finding out what happened to Kimmy is the truth, and I don't want to accept it."

"Nonsense. You need to keep going."

"And what if I find out that Kimmy is one of the refugees adopted? What do I do then? Fight for her? Screw her up even more than she already is? Damn it, why is life so cruel?"

"Now, now. Don't jump ahead. Let's take this nice and slow, so you can keep your wits about you."

When they entered Sasha's small office, a typed adoption report was waiting for them.

"What does it say?" Claire squeaked as she watched Sasha's eyes flit back and forth and up and down the page.

"Kimmy's not listed. She's not adopted."

Claire collapsed in a chair. "Okay. Okay, then."

Sasha sat opposite her. "So, we start fresh. Again."

Claire grunted. "Yes. Another processing center. Another state."

"I can help you reserve a flight and ensure you're pre-approved to visit upon your arrival. I assume you want to check out Long Beach first and, if needed, then move on to Washington?"

Claire nodded.

"Okay. Let me get to work. Why don't you get something

to eat and take a load off our feet?"

"I'm too stressed out to rest, Sasha."

"Then do something to take your mind off things, even for a little while."

****

Claire spent the afternoon wandering about Harmon Hall and soon found out there was much to see from the supply and demand side of the operation. For the first time since the accident, she wished she had a camera handy. After she'd returned home from Saigon, her parents had bought her a brand new camera with all the accessories. At the time, Claire was so deep in her misery she didn't have the heart to tell them that she'd lost total interest in photography. That she feared that if she even dared look through a camera's lens, she'd see nothing but bloody images from the crash scene.

"Claire!"

She turned at the sound of her name.

Sasha came running up to her. "I've been looking all over for you!"

"You told me to do something to take my mind off things. I tried to watch some slapstick comedy in the entertainment tent, but it only made me want to cry. So, I thought I'd just mosey about, taking in the sights."

Sasha wiped sweat from her brow. "I have great news."

Claire's heart skipped a beat. "Tell me."

Sasha's response was to hold up the list of hospitals from the day before. She grinned at Claire and turned it around. "Another hospital was listed on the reverse side of the list: St. Francis Memorial. We totally missed it."

Claire wondered if this could be the missing needle in the haystack.

"I just phoned them," Sasha said. "They told me that a female matching Kimmy's age and physical description, remains a patient in their burn ward. Get this, her name is Kiem Nuuan. Sounds pretty damn close, doesn't it?"

Chapter Nineteen

St. Francis Memorial Hospital lay nestled on three acres of rural land, with an abundance of sycamore and black walnut trees and landscaped gardens as its backdrop.

"Are you sure we're in the right place?" Claire asked, as Sasha backed the sedan into a parking space close to the entrance. "This looks more like a wealthy estate than a hospital. It's so peaceful and remote."

"The hospital's privately funded and uses state-of-the-art science and medical technology to treat burn victims."

"How did the girl get into a place like this?"

"The severity of her burns and, quite possibly, the financial aid of a Good Samaritan."

Once inside the hospital, Sasha made a beeline for the admissions desk to sign in while Claire waited beside a large fish tank.

Sasha returned in a flash. "Dr. Vale is the girl's attending physician. He's on level three, at the end of the hall. We can take the elevator."

As the elevator ascended, Claire's anxiety surged. "Sasha? What if this is another wild goose chase? What if the patient isn't Kimmy?"

"The question you should be asking yourself is, what if the patient is Kimmy? How great would that be?"

"It'd be a miracle."

Sasha winked. "I've been told that, on occasion, miracles do happen."

Once on level three, they walked in silence to the lone office at the end of the hall.

A man opened the office door before either Sasha or Claire could knock.

"Ms. McCallum? Ms. Mendez? Welcome. I'm Dr. Vale. I've been expecting your arrival."

Doctor Seymour Vale stood tall and lean, like a beanpole. He reminded Claire of Disney's animated version of

Ichabod Crane, the fictional schoolteacher from *The Legend of Sleepy Hollow.*

Vale ushered them inside and set to work clearing stacks of textbooks from two straight-backed chairs. "Please, have a seat, and don't mind the mess." Vale rounded his desk and settled into a plush office chair. He placed his elbows on the desktop, tented his fingers, and looked at them with eyes the color of blue diamonds. "It's my understanding that you're here to see Kiem Nuuan."

"Yes," Claire said. "We're hoping that she's the girl I know as Kimmy Nguyen."

"Kiem is a remarkable young girl. So strong and brave. An optimist through and through. I'm eager to hear how you both met."

Claire recounted she and Kimmy's past, ending with the crash and her cross-country search to find her.

"My Lord, you've survived a traumatic ordeal and an arduous quest for the truth," Vale said. "You should be commended for your efforts."

Claire glanced at Sasha. "I wouldn't have gotten this far without Ms. Mendez's help."

"Then bravo to both of you." Vale reached for a blue manila folder.

Therein lay the possible truth. Claire resisted the urge to snatch it from his hand.

Vale opened the folder. "Of course, due to patient confidentiality, I'm limited as far as to what I can tell you. However, I can give you a brief overview. Kiem survived the plane crash but suffered extensive burns to her lower extremities. My initial thought upon first meeting her was that it looked like she'd walked through the flames to escape. She also suffered facial scarring from flying shrapnel and the loss of sight in her right eye."

Claire clutched Sasha's hand in a vice-like grip.

Vale continued. "A rescue crew choppered her from the crash site back to the originating air base where medical staff worked round the clock to treat her for shock and monitor her vital signs. She was IV infused with hydrating fluids and antibiotics and, once stabilized, flown out on the second OBR flight stateside."

"What a blessing," Sasha said.

"Indeed," Vale said. "Upon Kiem's admission to St. Francis, we continued a more aggressive course of treatment with favorable results."

"You mean debridement, right? And skin grafting?" Claire fought down the urge to vomit. Her first aid training had taught her that debridement was the removal of all damaged skin from an affected area, which leaves the area raw and exposed. From there, healthy skin is removed from another part of the victim's body, a fattier part like a thigh or a buttock, and grafted on the affected area. It was a painfully excruciating procedure.

Whether this little girl was Kimmy or not, Claire's heart ached for her.

Vale lowered his spectacles to the tip of his nose. "You're familiar with these procedures?"

"I'm medically certified with the American Red Cross. I assisted in many debridement and tissue graft surgeries during my tour."

Vale continued. "I see. Well, it's refreshing to hear you have a medical background. I'm happy to report that Kiem is healing much better than expected. She's well out of the danger zone as far as any threat of infection. However, we've kept her on a low-dose antibiotic as a precaution. Kiem's last scheduled treatment is a short course of physical therapy to further strengthen her lower limbs. She may need a cane for balance for a month or so, but I have no doubt she'll make a full recovery."

"What happens then?" Claire asked.

"Why, she'll be transferred to Harmon Hall."

Claire voiced what she'd been holding back since first entering St. Francis. "Can we see her?"

Vale grinned. "By all means."

Claire, then Sasha, followed Vale out of his office and down a series of intersecting hallways. Vale's long strides forced them to quicken their pace to keep up. By the time they caught up with him at a set of double doors, both Claire and Sasha were panting from exertion.

Vale said, "Ladies, we're now entering the burn ward."

Claire cringed. She couldn't help it. How many more

burn victims was she going to have to see? Why did this have to keep happening?

Vale clearly noticed. "Again, ladies, I must remind you to hide whatever emotions you're experiencing from Kiem so as not to upset her. As it is, her sense of self is shaken from the trauma."

"Of course," Claire whispered. She took a deep breath in, then out. The pendant around her neck rose and fell with her breathing. After a series of ten inhalations and exhalations, her body calmed.

"I'll go in first, so I can prepare Kiem for your visit." The door opened with a soft swoosh and Vale entered, closing it behind him.

A split second later, Claire was up against the door, nose pressed against the top section of glass. "Damn. The bed's out of view. I can't see anything."

Sasha touched her shoulder. "It's okay. Vale will come out soon enough."

"Not soon enough for me. I'm dying from the suspense." She reached for the knob and drew her hand back when it turned on its own. When she looked up, she saw Vale scowling at her.

Claire retreated a few steps to allow him to come out.

"Ladies, I've told Kiem that some visitors have come to see her," Vale said.

"That's all? That we're just visitors? Not friends?" Claire asked.

"I assume she'll let us know to what extent your relationship is on her own."

"But, that's ridic—"

Sasha pinched her arm. "Claire, behave," she whispered. "He's being protective."

Claire clamped her lips shut and waited for Vale to again open the door. She'd ventured only a few feet into the room when, to her right, she spotted something that made her heart swell and her knees buckle. A satchel, *her* satchel, hanging from a wall hook. She looked farther right, saw a privacy curtain drawn across a hospital bed. Saw bandaged legs hanging over the side, swinging up and down, up and down. Claire forced her feet to move, even if only inches at a time. In a choked whisper Claire asked, "Kimmy? My dear, sweet girl? Is that you? Have you been waiting for me to find you all this time?"

At the sound of Claire's voice, the leg movement stopped and the curtains rustled. Claire extended her hand, felt the fabric brush against her fingertips. And something else. A slight pressure from the other side, pressing against her fingers. "It's okay, Kimmy. It's me. Claire. Má."

Claire took a deep breath and drew the curtain back.

And there sat Kimmy, her Kimmy, staring back at her wide-eyed and trembling with excitement.

What happened next played out in slow motion. There were shouts of joy and tears of happiness. There were giggles and hugs. Once reunited, nothing else, no one else, mattered. Without a word, Doctor Vale closed the door to give them privacy. Claire couldn't stop kissing Kimmy's forehead and cheeks. Their tears intermingled with their laughter. In their excitement, they both kept switching between speaking in English to speaking in Vietnamese. When Claire tried to pull away, Kimmy buried her face in her chest and held on as if for dear life.

"No, my sweet. I want to see your beautiful face, the face I've dreamed about every night since we've been apart."

Kimmy stiffened and covered the injured side of her face with her hand. She doesn't want me to see her scars, Claire realized. With the utmost tenderness, Claire reached for Kimmy's hand and pulled it away from her face. She cupped Kimmy's chin and raised it until their eyes met. Claire whispered. "You are so beautiful. So wanted. So loved."

Kimmy's bottom lip quivered. "I didn't think you would ever find me."

"Now, now, kiddo, you know me better than that. Nothing in the world could have kept me from finding you."

"And Maggie? Is Maggie with you?"

Claire breathed through a knot of pain that had settled in her belly.

"No, Kimmy. Maggie isn't here."

"But will she come later?"

"No." Claire hugged her tighter. *Why does life have to be so damn hard? Why does Kimmy have to suffer another loss? Hasn't she suffered enough?*

Claire pulled away so that she could look deep into Kimmy's eyes. "Kimmy… I have something very sad to tell you. Maggie didn't survive the crash. She's with the angels in heaven, looking over you. Looking over us. She's our guardian angel."

Kimmy's brow furrowed. "No, Maggie is alive. I saw her."

Claire sighed. *Denial. Kimmy's in denial much like I was for the past three months. Chances are, she's blocked out everything that happened after the plane crashed.*

"Yes, kiddo. We both did. In the moments before we boarded the plane."

Kimmy's expression hardened. "No. No. After. She helped me."

Damn it. Claire was upsetting her. Maybe now was not the time. "Okay, Kimmy. Okay, darling. You saw Maggie. She helped you. I get it. How about we talk later, okay? What I want for you right now is to rest up so that I can take you home."

Kimmy's cocked her head to one side. "Home? You're taking me back to Tan Son Nhut?"

"No, my dear, sweet Kimmy. I'm taking you to a place far more special. It's a place where I'm going to make all your dreams come true. Just you wait and see."

✳✳✳✳

Having to say goodbye to Kimmy until the following day tore at Claire's heartstrings. After so many months of not knowing if Kimmy was alive or dead, and now finding her safe and sound, Claire didn't want to be separated from her for not even a second. But rules were rules.

Vale escorted them to the hospital's main entrance.

"I cannot tell you how pleased I am to see Kimmy so happy," Vale said.

"That makes two of us," Claire said.

"Correction," Sasha said. "Three."

They shared a laugh.

"I do have a confession to make, though," Vale said. "When I learned of your full name from Ms. Mendez, I had a strong suspicion."

"Suspicion?"

"You must understand that I didn't want to jump to any conclusions. I mean, after all, coincidences do happen."

"You're losing me, Doc," Claire said.

"Over the course of her stay, Kiem's talked nonstop about a woman, Claire. And another woman, Maggie. Again, I didn't want anyone to have any false hopes, so I kept this information to myself. I had to make sure. Had to see it with my own eyes."

"And now?" Claire asked.

"Now, I can rest easy at night knowing Kiem will be well taken care of. And, the fact that you have a degree of medical experience is an added bonus."

Claire grinned. "You're damned right she will be. First thing I'm going to do when Kimmy's released is file adoption papers."

"And I'm going to handle the adoption process from start to finish," Sasha added.

"Well, that is excellent news. Excellent news, indeed. You two make such a dynamic duo. You both should start wearing capes," Vale said.

Claire laughed. "We may don capes, but never leotards."

Vale watched them get into their car and start the engine. Then, with a final wave goodbye, Sasha pulled out of the lot.

On the return drive to Harmon Hall, Claire couldn't sit still. Her mind was a thunder cloud of swirling thoughts. "Once Kimmy is home with me, I'm going to set her up with a child psychologist, to help her work through her emotional scars. I'm then going to have her scholastically tested to see if she can mainstream into first grade in September. And clothes...new clothes, of course. And then—"

Sasha giggled. "Geez Louise, Claire McCallum. You're a raging ball of energy."

Claire threw her head back and laughed. "Don't you

see, Sasha? I now have a purpose again. Kimmy is my purpose. Kimmy is my life, and I'm going to make it a damn special one at that."

"Since Vale said it could take a few weeks to a month for Kimmy's release, please feel free to stay on at Harmon Hall."

"Oh, no, I couldn't. It'd be too much of an imposition."

"Consider a roof over your head, a warm bed, and three square meals a day payment for helping me out with day-to-day activities."

Claire grinned. "Now, that's a deal."

"Glad to hear it. First things first, though. Please close your mouth because you're beginning to drool."

Chapter Twenty

July, 1975

"Are you sure you have everything?" Sasha asked, as she stood with Claire and Kimmy outside Harmon Hall's front gate.

"I think so," Claire said. "As far as luggage goes, I traveled out here light. If it weren't for you lending me clothes, I'd be running around Harmon Hall naked. I can pretty much say the same for Kimmy, too."

"Documents? Do you have the adoption papers and citizenship forms?"

Claire grinned. "Relax, Sasha. Nothing's changed since you asked me two minutes ago. There's an original and a copy in my bag. And you have copies on file here, at Harmon Hall, right?"

"In triplicate. I'm so relieved you can foster Kimmy while you wait for the adoption to go through."

"As always, I couldn't have done it with you, Sasha."

Claire shaded her eyes and peered down the street. "And it looks like our cab's arrived, right on time."

Sasha grunted. "I wish you would've let me drive you to the train station."

Claire patted her hand. "You've done more than enough already."

"Do you have enough fun activities to keep Kimmy amused? It's going to take close to a week to travel cross country."

"I don't care if it takes months." Claire leaned in to whisper in Sasha's ear. "There's no way in hell I'm putting Kimmy through the emotional torture of another plane ride."

"I totally dig it."

"And I've got enough arts and crafts in my satchel to last twice as long as the ride."

The cab pulled up to the curb with a screech of brakes.

Claire hefted the satchel onto her shoulder.

"Well, this is it."

Sasha sniffled. "Damn, this is the part I hate. The good-bye part."

"Agreed. But don't forget about what we talked about? Saying goodbye is not as if we're saying goodbye forever. Rather, we'll catch each other on the flip side, which means soon."

Sasha wiped tears from her eyes. "I remember."

Claire snapped her fingers. "I've got an idea. Maybe you can come out east and spend the holidays with us."

Sasha's eyes brightened. "I'd like that."

Claire hugged her. "Thank you, again. I could never have found Kimmy on my own."

"That's why we're the dynamic duo, right?"

"Damn right we are."

Sasha pulled away and dropped to one knee. "Kimmy, come here and give your Aunt Sasha a great big hug."

Ever the doting mother, Claire made sure Kimmy's grip on her cane was firm and that there were no cracks in the sidewalk to trip her. Kimmy adjusted her peace sign eye patch and shuffled forward.

"I will miss you, Sasha."

"Me, too, little one. "Sasha kissed her cheek. "You are such a special little girl. Such a brave little soul. Promise you'll take good care of Claire for me?"

Kimmy bobbed her head twice before stepping back and taking Claire's hand.

The trio stood staring at each other until the cabbie tooted the horn and revved the engine.

Once Claire and Kimmy were seated and belted in, Sasha closed the cab's rear door and stepped onto the curb. As the cab pulled away, Claire and Kimmy waved and blew kisses to her through the cab's rear window. Sasha returned the gestures until they disappeared from sight.

****

Grand Central Station – New York, New York

Claire had no sooner disembarked from the lounge car when a series of bright flashes accosted her, making her squint and lose focus.

"What the hell?"

A voice shrieked to her left. "Claire! Claire, darling! Over here!"

Claire didn't have to see clearly to know who was calling to her. Mom. Once her vision returned, she realized her mother was also the cause of the flashes. Claire looked closer at the camera she held in her hands and realized it was the one they'd originally bought her. Well, at least someone's enjoying it, Claire thought. Sherri snapped a few more shots before handing the camera off to Claire's dad and charging Claire with arms outstretched and tears streaming down her cheeks.

"Claire! Oh, Claire. My sweet baby. We've missed you so much."

Even though Claire disliked grandiose public displays of affection, this time she relented and let her mother hug and kiss her for all to see.

"Oh, Mom. Dad. I've missed you both so much. And I have so much to tell you. But first, there's someone very special I'd like you to meet."

Claire turned and raised her arms. Kimmy, who was standing on the train car landing, wrapped her arms around Claire's neck and let Claire lift her and set her down on the station platform inches from Sherri.

Sherri took one look at Kimmy and collapsed to her knees to cuddle her. "Kimmy! Our lovely grandchild. How adored you are." Sherri looked at her husband, who'd been standing a few feet away watching the reunion. "Mike, don't be nervous. Come here and say hello to our new granddaughter."

Claire smirked. "Go ahead, Dad. I promise she won't bite."

With an awkward smile, Mike stepped forward holding a colorful array of balloons and a large stuffed animal that resembled a rainbow-tinted unicorn. Claire burst into laughter at the awed expression on Kimmy's face when she spied the unicorn. It took her only a few moments to get over her shyness before accepting the toy and hugging it as if it were a lifelong friend.

As Sherri continued to fawn over Kimmy, Mike reached for his daughter's hand. "A new chapter awaits, Claire."

"Yes, Dad. A new chapter."

And the end of an old one. Claire's chest tightened. Maggie. Oh, Maggie. How could she start a new chapter without her?

****

September, 1975

Claire stepped out of the misty rain into the foyer of her parents' home. She hung her bright-yellow slicker on a wall hook and shook droplets of rain from her hair before moving into the living room.

"Hello? Anybody home?"

Her mother's cheery voice echoed from the sewing alcove near the kitchen. "Claire! You're home just in time."

Holding an armful of sheer pink fabric, Sherri met Claire halfway.

Claire scowled. "My God, what is that?"

"Why, it's a lace-trimmed canopy to go over Kimmy's bed."

"Of course it is. You know, Mom, if you're not careful, Kimmy's going to have you and Dad wrapped around her pinkie finger in no time."

"Oh, hush, Claire. A critical disposition doesn't become you." Sherri eyed Claire's attire. "What does become you, though, is that uniform. My, you look so professional. How was your first day of work?"

Claire looked down at her baby-blue, regulation American Red Cross pantsuit and smiled. "Out of sight! I think I've found my niche in becoming a recruitment officer. If I can't do humanitarian work overseas, I can sure as hell help out in any way I can on the home front."

Sherri wagged her finger at her. "Claire, mind your language."

"Oops. Sorry, Mom."

"Follow me upstairs. I can't wait to show you how I converted the spare bedroom into a princess-themed wonderland."

As they ascended, Claire wondered how her mother would react when the time came for her and Kimmy to move out on their own. Best not to think about that now. She had some saving to do before anything major like that happens.

Claire took one look inside the room and gagged. On opposite sides of a massive four-poster bed sat a dollhouse, a drawing desk, and a carousel-style rocking horse. But it wasn't the furniture or toys that had her stomach doing flip flops. It was the walls. "Mom, what were you thinking? You painted the walls the color of that horrible pink stomach medicine you poured down my throat when I was a kid. Are you trying to make Kimmy throw up, too?"

Sherri fluffed a unicorn-patterned pillow. "Oh, pshaw. It's the perfect color pink for our perfect little girl. After all, grandchildren, especially granddaughters, are for spoiling. And Kimmy's a good, old-fashioned girly-girl, unlike you."

"Uh-huh. Well, you'll be happy to hear that on my lunch hour, I made a phone call to Principal Wheaton at Hobarth Elementary School. He said that Kimmy tested high on the language and mathematical skills tests, so she can attend first grade, even though it's already a few weeks into the semester."

Sherri clapped. "Such fantastic news. Kimmy will be thrilled. Although she's crazy about me, I do realize that she needs to socialize with other children."

"Yes." Claire glanced around. "All of this talk of Kimmy reminds me."

"Of what, dear?"

"Where is Kimmy?"

"Your father took her to the park and then for ice cream."

Claire chuckled. "Like I said, wrapped around her pinkie finger."

"Claire..."

"Hmm?"

"How are you holding up? I know a lot's changed and, with no word about Maggie... Well, I worry about you."

"I'm okay, Mom. It's not easy coming to terms with another's death, but I can't live my life pining for a ghost. It would be so unfair to Kimmy."

"I suppose."

"But I do wish Maggie was here to see how far Kimmy's come. She would be so very proud of her."

Chapter Twenty-One

Claire clicked off her desk lamp and reached for her satchel. Quitting time. Finally, she could go home, settle back and relax. She hoped her father had restocked the fridge with beer. Just as she was about to leave the office, the phone rang. Claire frowned. Should she let it ring, or answer and risk missing the bus? Claire's strong sense of responsibility and willingness to help far surpassed getting out of the office on time. No phone call was unimportant. She picked up the clunky receiver. "Claire McCallum, American Red Cross Recruitment Office. How can I help you?"

"Claire, it's Mom."

Claire twirled the phone cord. "Hi, Mom. I'm on my way out. Do you need me to pick up anything from the market on my way home?"

"No, I need you to meet me at Doctor Miller's office."

Her mother's high-pitched tone had Claire's heart thudding hard against her ribcage. Dr. Miller. Kimmy's psychologist. "What wrong, Mom?"

"Nothing's wrong, dear. On the contrary, there's been a breakthrough."

"I'll be right over."

Claire rushed to catch the bus, only just barely making it. Breakthrough. What kind of breakthrough? And what did it mean as far as Kimmy's emotional well-being?

She nervously drummed her fingers on her leg for the entire ride. As her stop approached, she leapt up and yanked on the overhead cord to signal the bus driver to stop. The bi-fold doors had only partially opened when Claire squeezed through and hurried up the tree-lined street to Miller's office.

Dr. Miller and her mother were waiting for her on the wraparound front porch. Claire quickened her pace and took the porch steps two at a time. A pitcher of lemonade and three glasses sat on a table beside three Adirondack-style chairs.

Miller smiled and extended her hand. "Claire. I'm so glad to see you. Your mother tells me you've been doing admirable work for the American Red Cross."

Claire shrugged. "I'm trying."

"You're doing much more than trying. You're succeeding."

Claire felt as if she were about to jump out of her skin. She wanted to say, enough with the small talk, already, and tell me what the hell's going on. Instead, she asked, "Where's Kimmy?"

Miller motioned over her shoulder. "She's in the den watching cartoons. I thought it'd be wise to talk out here, away from prying eyes and elephant ears, if you know what I mean."

Once refreshments were poured and the women were seated and relaxed, Doctor Miller opened a file folder and slid out a sheet of white construction paper. She placed the paper on the table in front of Claire and Sherri.

"Kimmy drew two pictures for me during our session this afternoon. I find each so significant in meaning that I needed to see you both at once."

Claire leaned forward and inhaled sharply. The picture was a crude, colored drawing of a child, presumably Kimmy, being carried through flames by a woman with blonde hair and gray eyes. In the background were the charred remains of a crashed plane and many contorted, stick-figure bodies lying strewn on the ground.

Doctor Miller continued. "During the weeks of Kimmy's therapy, she's drawn numerous pictures depicting the plane crash. In these pictures, Kimmy drew herself either trapped in the plane unable to get out, or lying amongst the other victims, doomed to die."

Claire couldn't take her eyes off the crude figure of a woman cradling Kimmy in her arms. Maggie. My God, Kimmy's drawn Maggie.

"Claire, have I lost you?" Doctor Miller asked.

Claire blinked and brought her attention back to the

present. "I'm sorry, Doctor Miller. Please, go on."

"Kimmy's earlier drawings were her way of showing how desperate and helpless she felt in the moments after the crash. But then she drew herself being rescued by this fair-haired woman. This is a clear indication that Kimmy has moved past the traumatic ordeal of feeling helpless and afraid to finally accepting she is no longer in danger. Claire, do you know this woman in Kimmy's drawing?"

"Not sure," she lied. Claire couldn't think straight. Had Maggie not only survived the crash, but also rescued Kimmy? Was that even possible? And, if that were so, then Kimmy hadn't been wishfully thinking Maggie had survived. Maggie had, indeed, done just that.

Doctor Miller retrieved another piece of construction paper from the folder. In this drawing, Claire saw that Kimmy had drawn a stick figure of herself with arms outstretched toward a bright yellow sun.

"Kimmy drew this at the end of our session. The picture is significant in that Kimmy is drawing herself welcoming a new day. I believe Kimmy's overcome the worst of her trauma and is now ready to move into the light and promise of the future."

Sherri used a tissue to dab at her teary eyes. "Thank the saints above," she said.

Claire hadn't realized she'd been holding her breath until her throat constricted and she exhaled in a loud huff. She felt her mother's hand on hers. "Are you all right, dear?"

Claire forced a smile and nodded. It was the best she could do as her mind was filled with images of Maggie.

****

When dinner ended, Mike and Kimmy retired to the living room to play board games while Claire and her mother washed and dried dishes.

"You've barely said a word since we got home from Doctor Miller's," Sherri said.

Claire frowned. "Sorry, Mom. Today was...intense."

"It's the woman in the picture Kimmy drew, right? Is

that Maggie?"

Claire fumbled with a dish. "I don't know who else it could be."

"But then that would mean that Maggie had survived the crash and was strong enough to rescue Kimmy."

"Yes. Which would mean that Kimmy was telling me the truth all along. She wasn't fabricating what happened as a means of coping with the shock of the event itself. And I didn't believe her."

"Or, it could be just as you thought. She keeps drawing Maggie because she's still having trouble coming to terms with her being gone."

Claire wiped her hands on a dish towel. "I need to talk to her. And this time I need to listen. Listen hard to what she remembers."

Once the evening ritual of bath and story time ended, and Kimmy lay snuggled beneath a quilted comforter, Claire sat beside her and smoothed her shiny black hair.

"Kimmy?"

Kimmy looked up at her and smiled. She's so beautiful, Claire thought. I'm so fortunate to have her as my own.

"The picture you drew for Doctor Miller today of the woman carrying you."

"Maggie," Kimmy whispered, with a grin that could warm the coldest of hearts. "She helped me escape. She carried me away from the fire. But you tell me that she's in heaven now, and that she looks after me like a Garden Angel."

Claire took a deep breath to steady her nerves. Garden Angel. She means Guardian Angel. A pang of guilt roiled in her belly. How could she have been so wrong?

"Once in a while, Maggie comes to visit me and we play, and play, and play."

Claire gripped the mattress until her knuckles turned white. "Visit you? Where does Maggie visit you, Kimmy?"

"In my dreams."

Claire looked away so Kimmy wouldn't see her pained expression. "You are such a lucky girl to have Maggie visit you in your dreams."

Kimmy wriggled beneath the sheet. "Does Maggie visit

you in your dreams?"

Claire shuddered. The only time Maggie visited was in her nightmares. "Not the same way, Kimmy."

"Maybe, we can say a prayer and she will."

"Maybe."

Kimmy sat up and reached for Claire's hands. With eyes closed, Kimmy recited "Star light. Star bright. First star I see tonight. I wish I may. I wish I might. Have the wish I wish tonight." Kimmy opened her eyes. "Okay, Má. Now make a wish, but not out loud or it won't come true."

Claire wished for peace. Peace for a heart broken into a gazillion pieces. Her heart.

Once outside of the bedroom, Claire covered her mouth and succumbed to muffled weeping. Although surrounded by all of the people she loved, she'd never felt more alone.

****

November, 1975

Claire and Kimmy barged into the McCallum house like a pair of out-of-control revelers. Apparently startled by their raucous laughter, Sherri raced from the kitchen to the living room. She took one look at them and scowled. "I thought you said you were going to rake the leaves, not roll in them! Look at you both. You're covered from head to toe."

Claire and Kimmy pointed at one another at the same time. "She started it."

"I don't care who started it," Sherri said. "I'm finishing it. Outside, the both of you, to shake off. When you come in, take your shoes and socks off in the foyer. I just vacuumed."

When they returned inside a few minutes later, Claire and Kimmy found Sherri in the kitchen, preparing lunch.

"What are we having, Mom-Mom?" Kimmy asked.

"Tomato soup and grilled-cheese sandwiches."

"Yum," Kimmy shouted and scampered to a dinette chair.

"No sitting until you wash those grubby hands of yours," Sherri said, without turning from the stove.

Claire was about to join Kimmy at the kitchen sink when the wall-mounted phone rang. "I'll get it," she said. "McCallum household," Claire announced into the receiver.

"Good afternoon," a male voice sounded. "I'm calling for a Ms. Claire McCallum."

"Speaking."

"Hi, Ms. McCallum. My name is Jim Golden from Time Magazine."

"I'm sorry, Mr. Golden," Claire said, thinking she'd misheard him. "Did you say you're from Time Magazine? I mean *the* Time Magazine in New York?"

She heard Golden chuckle. "Yes, Ms. McCallum. I am one of the magazine's editors. I received your photographs."

"Photographs?" Claire asked. "What photographs?"

"The ones of the refugee children at play during their stay at Tan Son Nhut Air Force Base. One picture, in particular, has captured our interest so much that we wish to publish it in our upcoming Post-Vietnam issue. The close up shot of the Vietnamese girl."

The emotional walls that surrounded Claire began closing in, compressing her body and making it hard to breathe. Golden continued to speak, but his words sounded garbled and indistinct. With tremendous effort, Claire found her voice.

"Excuse me, Mr. Golden. May I ask how you acquired these photographs?"

"We received a large manila envelope with an enclosed note listing your name, home address, and phone number."

Claire felt a dense mental fog try to settle on her consciousness. Think, she silently commanded. Think, damn it.

"Mr. Golden, was there a return address on the envelope?"

"No, Ms. McCallum."

"Is there a postmarked location?"

Claire heard the rustle of papers. "Um, yes," Golden replied. "The postmarked address is Bethesda, MD."

Maryland? She didn't know anyone in Maryland. But she knew someone who might.

Chapter Twenty-Two

Claire's fingers trembled as she dialed the phone number written on a tattered piece of paper she'd kept in her nightstand for the past month.

Now that the moment was upon her, Claire was nervous. She hadn't had any contact with George since his discharge and was unsure how he'd react to her call after being MIA for so long.

After four rings, a gruff voice answered. "VFW Post 7447. How can I be of service?"

The sound of George's voice brought tears to her eyes and, for a few seconds, she couldn't speak.

"Hello? Hello? Anybody on the line?"

Claire cleared her throat. "Hey, old timer. Whatcha been up to?"

Silence, except for the sound of a Perry Como song playing in the background.

"George? It's me. Claire."

George grunted. "Ah, the long lost sheep finally returns home hoping to be welcomed back into the fold."

"Is that how you think of me? As being lost?"

"Not as much as being lost, but not wanting to be found."

"I'm sorry."

"No apologies. I reckon you have your reasons."

"Would you like to hear them? My reasons?"

"Sure. It's a slow night at the post, and I could use the distraction."

A short time later, Claire finished recounting her past ordeal. She'd decided ahead of time that she wouldn't go into any explicit detail about her relationship with Maggie. Her coming-out story would have to wait for another day.

George let out a haggard breath. "Damn, Claire. All this time I thought you'd forgotten me."

"Never."

"I had no idea you were involved in Operation Baby Rescue."

"It was a top-secret operation. After the crash, I kind of lost it for a while. Mentally and physically. It took some time for me to come around. Hell, I'm still not fully right in the head. I get dizzy spells sometimes. And dull headaches. They're supposed to ease in time, but we'll see."

"The important thing is that you're safe. Time will heal the rest of it."

"I'm proud of you, George. You did it. You got your own VFW Post up and running. How does it feel?"

"Like I've taken my own slice of military life with me. Day in and day out, former soldiers come in to have a few drinks, share a few laughs, and rid their minds of haunted memories. I'll tell you, Claire, their battle scars may be old, but the memories of how they got them are as fresh as an open wound."

"And Dickey?"

George guffawed. "Hell, he's the proverbial thorn in my side. We run this place together. He's got a nasty cold, so I sent him home so he wouldn't snot all over the patrons. He's going to raise all kinds of hell because he missed your call."

"I'll catch up with him next time."

"Better yet, come out for a visit. I've got a studio apartment in the back that has its own bathroom and kitchenette. It's not the Ritz Carlton, but it's clean and tidy."

Claire smiled into the receiver. "I'd like that very much. But..."

"Ah, I knew there had to be another reason why you contacted me. Out with it, little lady."

"I need your help."

"In what way?"

"I need to find someone."

"Someone? Is this someone a he, or a she?"

"She."

"Hm. Has she done you wrong?"

"Maybe."

"Are you out for revenge?"

"No. I'm out for closure."

"Tell me more."

"She's a captain in the Air Force. Her full name's Margaret Anne Calder. The Anne is spelled with an *e*."

"Yeah, I remember her. Tall, blonde. She was your commanding officer, right?"

"Yes. She was on the Goliath, too."

"Did she survive? I know there are a hell of a lot of victims who are still not identified."

"For the longest time I felt certain she'd died, but now I'm not so sure. Call it a gut instinct."

"Then why hasn't she reached out to you?"

"That's what I need to find out. I remember you once saying you have connections in many branches of the armed forces."

"I do, indeed."

"Will you help me? I think I may have a lead. In Maryland."

"Sure. Give me an hour or two to poke around, and I'll get back to you. What's your number?"

It took George less than an hour to call her back. "You're in luck. I got in touch with an old buddy of mine who's second in command at the Veterans for Foreign Affairs Administration. I gave him the info on your missing friend. He was able to track her down in the time it took for me to take a piss. Uh, excuse my French."

Claire's chest tightened, and her breathing strained. "Is she...? Is Maggie dead?"

"Hell, no. Your Captain Calder is alive and kicking. And you were right about your possible lead. She heads the Medical Services Division of the largest VA hospital in Bethesda, MD."

"Oh, my God!" Claire's hands began to shake with shock, and she lost her grip on the receiver. She caught it by its coiled cord before it hit the ground. Maggie was alive? And she'd never contacted her? How is that even possible? A fireball of rage burned in her gut, spreading ever outward.

"Claire, are you okay?"

"I'm losing my shit here, George. In my eyes, the sun rose and set on this woman. We were soul mates. Partners in every sense of the word. George—George, I *loved* her. There has to be a mistake."

"There's no mistake on official paperwork, Claire. Your Captain Calder is, indeed, working for the VA Hospital in Maryland. I'm sorry."

"But—"

"Look, I know all this comes as a shock, but I need to tell you something before you go off half-cocked."

She barely heard him. A question kept revolving in her head, like a record album with a phonograph needle stuck in its groove. Maggie! How could you? How could you? How could you? Her grip tightened on the receiver until her fingers ached.

"Claire! Are you listening to me?"

George's harsh tone brought her attention back to the present. "Yes. Yes."

"Claire, passion runs deep and it doesn't matter whether it's anger, or love, or envy, or the rest of the emotions that rule us. What does matter is how a person goes about dealing with these emotions when in the heat of a stressful moment."

"Is this your roundabout way of telling me to think before I react?"

"Yes. I'd hate to see you act out of character and then regret it."

Claire felt burning heat coursing through her veins. "I promise not to do great bodily harm."

"You're not funny. I'm serious. No good comes from loss of temper."

Claire's shoulders sagged. "Okay. Okay. I'm just so...blown away."

"Promise me you won't fly off the handle. That you'll think everything through before you do anything."

"On my honor, George. I promise."

Claire hung up the phone and began to pace her room. At last, the jumbled puzzle pieces were falling into place. And as the pieces fell into place, they formed a picture, a reality Claire hadn't ever imagined. Maggie was alive, living her life independently from them. She abandoned us. Left us to wallow in our heartbreak. How could she deceive them so? Deceive Claire? What type of heartless person does something like that? And then Claire remembered. A black-hearted person does that. A cold, black-hearted person. And one who once wore a pendant to prove it.

Claire grabbed the telephone off her night stand, ripped its cord from the wall outlet, and hurled the device across the room, shattering a mirror.

Within seconds, Sherri raced into Claire's bedroom. "Sakes alive, Claire. What is going on in here? Did you have one of your dizzy spells and fall into the mirror? Are you hurt?"

Claire covered her face to hide her tears. "Go away, Mom."

Sherri moved to her side. "I will do no such thing. All I can say is that it's a good thing Kimmy's on a playdate over at the neighbor's and your Dad's working late. We can have this mess cleaned up in no time, and no one would be the wiser."

When Claire dropped her hands, Sherri cried out, "Claire, you're as white as a sheet. Are you ill?" She placed her palm against Claire's forehead. "You don't seem to be running hot. Should I call Doc Woodruff?"

Claire shook her head.

"Then, sweetie, please tell me what's wrong."

"I found her, Mom. I found Maggie. She's alive."

Sherri gawked at her. "Alive? Why, that's wonderful news, Claire."

Claire wiped snot from her nose with the back of a hand. "She's more than alive, Mom. She's alive and well, living in Maryland."

Sherri's eyes narrowed and her smile turned into a frown. "You mean..."

"Yes. She's forgotten about me, Mom. Forgotten about Kimmy, too."

Sherri lowered herself onto the edge of the bed and wrung her hands. "What are you going to do?"

"Drive down there. Confront her. Find out the truth."

"When?"

"First thing tomorrow morning."

"Do you think that's wise, dear? So soon? Maybe you need to take a few days to process everything."

Claire grunted. That sounded like George's advice.

Thanks, but no thanks. "I'm afraid that if I allow myself to process too long, I might lose my nerve. You'll make sure Kimmy gets to school?"

"Of course. And picked up, and whatever else you need."

"I promise to be home in time for dinner."

Sherri teared up. "Maybe this is all a big misunderstanding. Maybe Maggie has good reason for not contacting you."

Claire squeezed Sherri's shoulders. "Thanks for the pep talk, Mom, but I don't think it's going to turn out that way."

"So why are you going? Why are you going to put yourself through the pain?"

"I need to look Maggie in the eyes and ask her why. Only then can I make peace with the past and find closure."

Sherri pulled a tissue out of the cuff of her blouse and blew her nose. "Then Godspeed, Claire. Godspeed."

Chapter Twenty-Three

Walter Reed Medical Hospital – Bethesda, MD

Claire showed her credentials at the reception desk. Upon receiving instructions, she accessed the nearest elevator and hit the number five. During the four-hour drive, she'd rehearsed over and over what she was going to say when she came face-to-face with Maggie Calder. To her mounting frustration, the imaginary scenes she played out in her mind always ended up with her breaking down and curling up in a fetal position at Maggie's feet.

But she had to be strong. She couldn't show emotion. Emotion was weakness. Claire was angry and she was hurt. She was a woman truly scorned. And she needed to know the extent of the emotional damage to Claire and Kimmy.

Claire hadn't realized she'd been lost in thought until the elevator bell sounded and its doors opened onto a narrow hallway. Yet again, a moment of truth had arrived. Claire took a deep breath, squared her shoulders, and moved forward.

A young, female aide met her in the reception area of a glass-paneled office.

"Good morning. My name is Geraldine. Can I help you?"

"I'm here to see Captain Calder."

"Your name, please?"

"Claire McCallum."

When Geraldine glanced down at her desk, Claire spoke again. "You won't find my name in your appointment book. You see, Captain Calder and I served closely together at Tan Son Nhut. I was hoping to surprise her with an unannounced visit."

Geraldine frowned. "I'm afraid Captain Calder isn't keen on unannounced visits."

"Please," Claire said. "I've come a long way to see her."

As if sensing Claire's desperation, Geraldine shrugged.

"It's close to lunchtime, after all. I keep telling Captain Calder that she shouldn't skip meals. Maybe you can draw her away from her desk long enough for a bite to eat?"

Claire forced a smile. Right now she would like to feed Maggie, piece by piece, to a bunch of starving alligators. "It'd be my pleasure."

"Captain Calder's office is down that hall, third on the right. Don't forget to knock first."

****

Claire knocked once, then twice. She'd almost turned tail and fled when Maggie's voice called out, "Come in."

Steeling herself for the worst, Claire turned the knob and entered.

And before her sat Maggie Calder, behind an expansive desk. Her head was lowered, and she was rifling through a stack of papers.

Claire was uncertain how long she stood staring before Maggie looked up. There was an immediate flicker of recognition in Maggie's eyes. Other than that, Maggie showed no emotion. Her expression was stone-faced and her eyes were as black as coal. A few beats of tense silence elapsed before Maggie spoke. "I knew it'd only be a matter of time before you found me."

Claire bridled. "Knew?"

"Sensed."

"You've been hiding out here? In some VA hospital all this time?"

"Yes. I thought it best to keep a low profile."

Rage consumed Claire. "Low profile? What the hell for?"

"To delay this moment for as long as I could."

"What the fuck, Maggie? All this time you've been alive, and you never once reached out to me to find out if I survived the crash? If Kimmy survived the crash?"

Maggie sighed. "I knew this was going to be difficult."

Claire resisted the urge to go off on a rip-roaring tantrum. Instead, she balled her hands into fists and dug her heels deeper into the carpet. "You're damned right it's going to be difficult. I thought you were one of the missing, or one of the many unrecognizable victims who died at the crash scene. Dammit, I mourned for you. I mourned for us!"

So much for controlling her temper. Sorry, George.

Claire hadn't realized she'd raised her voice until she saw Geraldine appear in the office doorway.

"Captain Calder?" Geraldine asked. "Is there a problem?"

Maggie smiled to reassure her aide. "Everything's fine, Geraldine. I suggest you take your lunch hour."

When Geraldine hesitated, Maggie said, "It's okay. Go."

Alone again, Maggie sighed. "Let's get a few things straight, Claire. I did my research. I knew you survived the crash and had returned home to your family to recuperate. I also knew that Kimmy was alive because I physically pulled her from the wreckage and handed her off to a rescue worker. I did my duty. I made sure you were both safe."

"And that was it? Then you erased the slate clean and moved on?"

"Not totally. Miraculously, my duffel survived impact, and I was able to send those photo negatives of Kimmy to Time magazine. I thought you deserved the recognition."

Claire rolled her eyes. "Oh, well, how thoughtful of you. What I want to know is when did you decide that I was unworthy of your love?"

Maggie shrugged. "Claire, people change. Feelings change."

"So, life goes on, right? Nice knowing you? Don't let the door hit you in the ass on your way out?"

"If you wish to put it so bluntly then... Yes."

Outraged, Claire reached for the ruby pendant that hung about her neck. She ripped the necklace free and hurled it at Maggie. "Fuck you, Maggie Calder! Fuck you to hell and back. I don't care if I never see you again."

Claire stormed out of Maggie's office and never looked back.

****

Claire returned home to find Sherri and Kimmy standing side-by-side at the kitchen table, both wearing matching aprons. Sherri was dropping globs of cookie batter onto a greased aluminum sheet while Kimmy sprinkled powdered sugar on a batch taken fresh from the oven.

Although seething with rage over her encounter with Maggie, Claire put her best face forward and said, "Yum! It smells delicious in here."

Hearing Claire's voice, Kimmy ran to her with batter-covered hands. "Yay! You're home in time for dessert."

Claire ruffled her hair. "Sorry I missed dinner, kiddo."

Sherri wiped her hands on a dishtowel and placed her hands on Kimmy's shoulders. "Why don't you shoo for a minute, Kimmy, and wash those hands."

Kimmy looked at her grandmother with adoring eyes. "You promise not to eat any without me?"

Sherri kissed her forehead. "I promise, not even one little nibble."

When Kimmy scampered from view, Sherri held out her arms and Claire moved into her embrace.

"Is it over?" Sherri asked.

"Yes, Mom. It's over. I promise I'll never shed another tear over such a lost cause."

****

February, 1976

Claire licked the back flap of an envelope and neatly stacked it with a pile of others. Bleh. Whatever glue they used as a seal was nasty. She really needed to buy herself a sponge. A glance at her watch showed there was fifteen minutes until she could clock out. She thrummed her fingers on her desk top and looked around the ARC Recruitment Office. There was still work to do. She could hang those new recruitment posters. Do some filing. And there was that damned Christmas tree her coworkers were so gung ho on putting up the day after Thanksgiving, yet were nowhere to be found to take it down. Claire grumbled, "I hate the holidays."

As soon as the words were out, she wanted to take them

back. Granted, the holidays had been trying, but Kimmy's innocence and excitement had brightened Claire's spirit to the point where she gave up on acting Scrooge-like and bah humbugging the last two months of the year away.

And now Valentine's Day was upon them. A day for lovers. Claire scoffed. Fuck lovers. Fuck love. It's all just a bunch of crap, anyway.

The bell chimed over the front door. Damn. A visitor. So much for getting out on time. She turned and gasped.

Mary Kate Bunsen stood in the doorway dressed in full ARC uniform. "Yoo hoo! Remember me?"

Claire blinked. "Buns! I mean, Mary Kate! How are you?"

Mary Kate closed the door behind her and wiped a few droplets of rain from her shoulders. "Well, as you can see, I arrived safely back home from Vietnam a little world weary and a little heavier than when I went."

"I...I...didn't—"

"Didn't expect me, right? Well, of course you didn't. How could you?"

Mary Kate chuckled, which made her bosom shake in time with her blonde ringlets. Claire found herself staring at a burgundy lipstick stain on Mary Kate's front tooth. Some things never changed.

Mary Kate glanced about the office, bobbing her head and smiling like a jack-in-a-box sprung loose. "Very nice atmosphere. Very nice, indeed. And clean and orderly. I like that."

Claire motioned to a chair. "Would you like to sit down?"

"No. No, I'm due in a conference at any minute."

"What brings you here? To New York? When you're from...Boise, right?"

Mary Kate beamed. "Such a great memory you have! Yes, I am a ways from home, but it's for dual purposes. One, I'm charged with assessing ARC sites on the east coast to make sure they are running and up to par. And, two, to give you great news!"

Claire furrowed her brow. "News? You're not here to talk me into again serving abroad, are you?"

"No, dear. I'm here to invite you to an upcoming memorial ceremony to be held at Arlington National Cemetery in Virginia in April."

"Memorial ceremony?"

"Why, yes. The ceremony is to commemorate one year to the day since Operation Baby Rescue launched. When I brought the Time magazine article to my supervisor, she all but busted a gasket. Neither she nor I, for that matter, knew that you were involved in the mission."

"It was top-secret."

"Well, it isn't any more, and your efforts are to be commended at the upcoming ceremony."

Efforts? What efforts? When Goliath crashed, she did nothing but lie on the ground and watch the fires of hell burn everything and everyone around her.

"Claire, dear? Are you listening?" Mary Kate asked.

Claire shook her head. "Yes. Yes."

"Now, I won't take no for an answer. This is a momentous occasion, and I want you there front and center, representing the American Red Cross. Oh, and please bring the child as well. Such a dear you are to give her a loving home when so many are still displaced."

Mary Kate moved forward and handed Claire an envelope. "Here is your official invitation. You are free to invite whoever you so choose. And, as the English say, ta ta for now!"

Chapter Twenty-Four

April 4, 1976 - One Year Post-Crash

"How do I look?" Claire stood before her parents and Kimmy wearing her regulation, baby-blue and white American Red Cross uniform with all the trimmings.

"You look radiant, Claire. Purely radiant," Sherri said.

Claire smoothed the front of her blouse. "I'm a bundle of nerves."

Mike patted her shoulder. "It's okay, honey. I know you're not one who likes being in the spotlight, but this is different. This is an honor. A privilege."

Claire nodded. "I know, Dad, but I don't have an acceptance speech written. I feel as if I'm flying by the seat of my pants."

Sherri plucked at an imaginary speck off Claire's tunic. "Just imagine everyone in the audience in their underwear."

Claire laughed in spite of her upset. "That's silly, Mom."

Sherri jutted out her chin. "Worked for me at all of those PTA meetings I headed."

"Uh-huh." Claire looked down at Kimmy. "What about you, kiddo? Does Má look spiffy?"

"Spiffy! Very spiffy!" Kimmy grinned and spun around, showing off her pink and white sundress with white, patent-leather shoes. "And me, Má?"

Claire ruffled her hair. "Absolutely gorgeous."

Mike tapped his index finger on the face of his wristwatch. "Okay, enough with the primping and preening. Are we ready to get this show on the road?"

Claire reached for her ARC cap. "Ready."

"Good. Then I'll get the car and pick you all up out front. We'd hate to be late for the ceremony."

****

Arlington National Cemetery, Virginia

Upon arriving at the gates of Arlington Cemetery, a valet hustled forward to park the McCallum's wood-paneled station wagon while two uniformed guards escorted them to the presentation stage and seated them in the front row.

Claire gawked at her surroundings. "My God, Mom. This place is magnificent. So peaceful. All the tree-lined paths, the floral gardens. It's heavenly."

Sherri nodded off in the distance to row upon row of white marble burial markers set on well-tended lawns and surrounded by majestic elm trees. "Yes, and sobering as well." They sat silent for a moment in quiet reflection.

Mike nudged Claire. "Check out that table over there. I've been told that Time Magazine donated a slew of commemorative magazines and had all your photos framed for display."

Claire shivered.

"Are you cold, dear?" Sherri asked.

"No, just feeling overwhelmed. This all seems so real."

"Because it is real. This is such an historic occasion. Your dad and I are so proud of you."

"Me, too!" Kimmy chimed in.

Sherri leaned in for a squeeze. "Thank God you're first on the award's agenda. It'll be over before you know it, and then you can relax with your friends."

"Friends?"

"Why, of course." Sherri turned in her seat and scanned the growing crowd. She smiled and waved. "Oh, there he is."

"There who is?"

Claire followed Sherri's line of vision and gasped. "Is that George?"

"In the flesh. And Sasha should be around here somewhere, too. Such delightful people."

"But how?"

"Well, I know you didn't want to make a big deal about it, but I did. So, I decided to invite them on my own."

A male voice droned over a loudspeaker "Ladies and gentlemen, if we could all please be seated, the afternoon ceremony is about to commence."

Moments later, an elderly woman dressed in ARC uniform strode across the stage to the outdoor microphone.

"Good afternoon. My name is Registered Nurse Charlene Wentworth, and it is my pleasure to stand before you today as a representative of the American Red Cross. As you know, our organization was founded by Clara Barton in 1881. She served as a nurse tending to the wounded in the American Civil War before continuing a long history of involvement in the women's suffragette movement and the pursuit of civil rights. And, in following in Ms. Barton's footsteps, the American Red Cross has grown by leaps and bounds and is now known worldwide for its humanitarian efforts both at-home and abroad. It is today that we come to honor one of our own: ARC Interpreter, Claire McCallum. Claire, amongst many other military personnel, medical workers, and refugee children was on board the fated Goliath when it crashed one year ago today. Although one of many survivors, we honor Miss McCallum today for her role in the ARC relief effort."

Wentworth motioned for Claire to come forward.

Claire rubbed clammy hands on her skirt and stood. "Here goes nothing," she whispered before stepping onto the stage to the applause of the crowd. Wentworth and Claire shook hands.

To Claire's surprise, Mary Kate Bunsen bustled on stage carrying a large plaque. She flashed Claire a wink and a smile before handing the plaque to Wentworth and then standing off to the side.

Wentworth began. "On behalf of the American Red Cross, it is my privilege to present Claire McCallum, American Red Cross Interpreter, with the American Red Cross Legacy Award. This award recognizes Red Cross staff and volunteers who have served side by side with members of the United States armed forces. Congratulations, Claire McCallum."

Claire clutched the commendation in both hands and bowed her head so that the audience couldn't see the tears welling in her eyes. Wentworth touched her shoulder. "Claire, would you like to say a few words?"

Claire swallowed past the golf ball in her throat. "I would."

"Good afternoon."

Another round of applause erupted and Claire waited for it to die down before she continued. "I thank the American Red Cross for this commendation. I stand here today as a loyal servant who has tried with all my heart to promote the common good and strive for peace. I have done everything in my power to uphold the seven fundamental principles the American Red Cross instilled in me, which are: humanity, neutrality, impartiality, independence, voluntary service, unity, and universality. At times, I know I've fallen short of my goals, but my failure has only served to push me forward to do better. I don't know why I made it out alive from the crash, when so many others didn't. Maybe the expression on a wing and a prayer might have had something to do with it. But I do know, that in their memory, I will continue to serve my country and tell their stories because they are the true heroes. And, as true heroes, they shall never be forgotten."

When she returned to her seat, both Sherri and Mike bear-hugged her. "You did wonderful, dear," Sherri said. "For sure, you're going to be a hard act to follow."

Claire blushed. "Aw, Mom..." She stopped and looked around. "Hey, where's Kimmy?"

"Kimmy? Why she was just here a second ago," Mike said.

Sherri stood and glanced about. "Oh, there she is, dear. Walking toward that huge elm tree."

Claire shaded her eyes and followed her mother's gaze. "You stay here, Mom. I'll go get her." Claire hurried toward Kimmy, who had managed to move quite a distance away from the presentation stage. When Claire was certain she was out of earshot and wouldn't disturb the ceremony, she hissed. "Kimmy. Hey, Kimmy. Hold up."

Kimmy stopped and turned toward the sound of Claire's voice.

Claire trotted the remaining distance that separated them. "Hey, what's up, kiddo? You know better than to go anywhere by yourself."

"I saw her, *Má*."

"Saw who?"

"Maggie. I saw Maggie."

Claire's insides churned and hot bile rose in her throat. Oh, no. Not again. I thought we were coming to terms with the fact that Maggie is no longer part of our lives.

"Kimmy..."

Kimmy startled Claire by grabbing her hands and yanking her forward. "I did. You must believe me. You must."

When Kimmy started to cry, Claire relented. "Okay. I'll go check it out. But you go back to Mom-Mom and Pop-Pop right this instant."

Claire groaned. This was a fool's errand. But true to her word, she trudged up a steep incline toward the top of where the row of grave markers began. From there she looked down. And saw a woman with blonde hair the color of spun silk seated in a wheelchair traveling along an asphalt path.

Not for the first time in her life did time stand still. It's her. Kimmy's right. It's Maggie. Claire's heart thudded painfully against her chest. And she's in a wheelchair.

"Stop!" Claire shouted. "Maggie, stop!"

Claire watched as Maggie's hands worked harder to propel the chair's oversized wheels. And then, suddenly, the wheelchair hit a patch of uneven ground and Maggie fell forward.

"Jesus!" Claire screamed and took off running toward her.

When she reached her, Maggie was struggling to get back into the wheelchair. Claire pressed on her shoulders to keep her in place.

"My God, Maggie. Don't move. Are you hurt?"

"Damn it. Damn it. Damn it," Maggie said. "I didn't want you to see me like this. I took every precaution for you to not see me like this. Or Kimmy."

"I don't understand."

Maggie slammed a fist into a mound of grass. "I shouldn't have come, but I had to see you shine."

Claire stared at her. "I thought you didn't want to have anything to do with me."

"After what I've been through. After the accident... I

thought it best not to put you or Kimmy through any further hardship.”

“Maggie, you’re not making sense. You need to tell me everything right now.”

“You mean the truth that I tried my damnedest to hide within a lie?”

“Everything. I want to hear everything. You owe me at least that.”

“Then sit down beside me.” Maggie ran trembling fingers through her hair. “Phew. This is hard.”

Claire gripped Maggie’s hand. “Please, go on.”

Maggie’s voice faltered and tears streamed down her cheeks. Finally, a crack in the dam.

“After the crash, after I saved Kimmy, I went to help the other injured children. Something exploded and part of Goliath’s fuselage broke free. I was trapped beneath it. The rest is foggy, but I eventually ended up in a Saigon hospital and was told my diagnosis. From that moment forward, I wanted to disappear and be left alone. Hell, there were dark times when I wished I hadn’t survived the crash. That I had been left there to perish with the others.”

“What diagnosis?”

Maggie ran her hands up and down her legs. “As you can see, I didn’t survive the crash unscathed.”

“You mean…”

Maggie grunted. “Yes. I’m paralyzed from the waist down.”

Through a haze of disbelief, Claire managed to ask, “Permanently?”

“Afraid so. The fuselage weight compressed my spine and caused extensive nerve damage. The doctors don’t hold out much hope of my ever regaining control of my legs.”

“Oh, my dear, sweet Jesus. Maggie, how could you have kept this from me?”

“I didn’t want you to have to bear the burden of taking care of me. That wouldn’t be fair.”

Claire’s anger flared and she fought it back. “No, you’re wrong. Not being fair is not telling me about your injury. Your hiding it from me behind that huge desk. Christ, I never imagined the day that I confronted you that you were sitting in a wheelchair."

"How could you have known? And I am so very sorry for how horribly I treated you. But do you now understand why I did what I had to do? I was doing it to protect you. To protect Kimmy. I didn't want either of you to face a lifetime of grief over any sense of displaced loyalty."

Tears clouded Claire's vision. She cupped Maggie's chin. "Maggie, don't you get it? You are my life. For me, not being with you, holding you, and touching you is damning me to a lifetime of grief. You didn't get to make the decision for me."

"Do you mean it?"

Claire rested her head on Maggie's shoulder. "I do. I love you, Maggie. I will always love you. That part's never changed, although I tried like hell to forget you. I really did."

Maggie nodded. "Trying to block you and Kimmy from my thoughts has been a living nightmare. It is only now, with you beside me, that I believe I can have a second chance at life. At love. Will you let me have that chance?"

Claire grazed Maggie's lips with her own. "Yes. God, yes."

They sat silently next to each other until their tears subsided.

Maggie reached for Claire's hand. "Damn, what a journey we've been through."

"Yes."

"And, after all is said and done, we succeeded at more than just surviving a war," Maggie added.

"Huh?"

"We've both come full circle. We set out to make a difference in this world and I do believe we've accomplished just that."

Claire grinned and wiped warm tears from her cheeks. "Yes, I finally feel at peace with my past, as if a heavy weight has finally been lifted from my shoulders."

Claire stood and righted the wheelchair. "Enough with wasting any more time. Let's see about getting you back in this wheelchair. I have some very special people for you to meet who would love to give us a homecoming celebration."

Maggie's eyed clouded over. "That is, if they'll accept me. After all that I've put you and Kimmy through."

"Nonsense. Now, you push up with your arms and I'll pull."

As Claire wheeled Maggie toward the presentation stage, they saw the audience stand in unison for the 'Pledge of Allegiance'. They hesitated for a split second. Although both knew from first-hand experience that their country wasn't perfect, they still honored its beliefs and would continue to serve. So, with right palms flat against left chests, they joined in.

"I pledge allegiance, to the flag, of the United States of America. And to its republic, for which it stands, one nation, under God, indivisible, with liberty and justice for all."

Epilogue

Syracuse, New York – One Year Later

Loud thumping, followed by raucous laughter, echoed down the hall to where Claire had turned a spare walk-in linen closet into her makeshift darkroom. She sighed. *They're at it again.* She used tongs to remove the last eight-by-ten, glossy black-and-white print from the developing fluid tray and hang it by a clip on a thin clothesline to dry. She wiped her hands on a rag poking out of the back of her Lee jeans, turned off the dim red safelight, and left her cramped confines.

She blinked at the bright daylight streaming in from the living room window. Not for the first time did she take a moment to reflect on how she'd come to this point in her life, how all of them had, and how all now stood tall in the present with a future shining as bright as a nova.

Crash. Then silence. Then another outburst of giggles.

Claire smiled in spite of her annoyance. "Kimmy? Quan? Stop breaking our house. Má Two isn't going to be happy if she has to fix another piece of furniture because you two won't stop roughhousing."

Two voices responded in unison. "Yes, Má."

Claire smiled. What a year it had been. After finally being reunited, Maggie had requested a transfer to Hancock Air Force Base in Syracuse, New York, working in their aerial logistics and topography department. The military put them up in a charming ranch-style home, equipped with handicap ramps and bars, within walking distance to the base. The commute was less than one half hour by car from the base to Claire's parent's front door and Claire's ARC office. Kimmy was also able to remain at Hobarth Elementary, and every Sunday there stood a standing dinner date at the senior McCallums.

A few months into living together, Claire brought up the idea of adopting another Vietnamese orphan to Maggie to help offset all the changes in Kimmy's life. They chose a boy named Quan as he was the same age as Kimmy, and they had kind of hit it off when at Tan Son Nhut. Neither Claire nor Maggie regretted their choice. Now, their love for one had blossomed into love for two.

Maggie had surprised her the following Christmas with having her grandmother's ruby pendant set in a gold ring, surrounded by small diamonds. Claire never took it off.

Old friends showed up at practically every holiday to visit and partake in the McCallum's family traditions. Even Sal came out once or twice a year when he wasn't on some top-secret reconnaissance mission. Sasha made damn sure that whenever she decided to pop in, she'd be welcome and the same held true for George.

Now, as winter ceded to spring, and the promise of warmth and rebirth hung heavy in the air, Claire thought back on everything she had done to aid in humanitarian efforts abroad, and everything that still remained left to do. With Maggie by her side, there was nothing out of their reach. Long ago, Claire realized that to have a purpose in life is essential, but to fulfill that purpose is golden.

THE END

About the Author

Barbara has been writing fiction in the psychic/supernatural, suspense/mystery, and horror/thriller genres since the mid-1970s. Her free time (when not writing, of course) is spent enjoying her family an friends, and any activities that involve being on, under, or near the ocean, for that is where she feels most in tune with her emotions.

Other Books By Barbara Valletto

Pulse Points

Do you dream of a lover who can transcend time and place? Who will protect you from harm at any cost? Or avenge you if evil has gotten to you first? Do you believe in total surrender of mind, body, and spirit for the sake of fighting forces of evil? If so, you will tread a fine line between what you believe to be morally just and what is only achieved by vengeance. You will face your own mortality and thirst for a chance at a higher level of being. Are you ready to meet her? She's been waiting…

The normally quiet town of Verhoven, NY, is plagued by a series of gruesome murders, leading Sheriff Lea Carlson to believe a serial killer is in their midst. Just when she thinks circumstances can't get any worse, Kylie Vinson, Lea's former lover, returns to Verhoven.

Kylie, a criminal behaviorist, has returned to Verhoven to find healing after surviving a brutal physical assault. But when Kylie is the one to find a murder victim, she and Lea put aside their unresolved feelings for each other to track down the killer.

Maya Holworth, Verhoven's newest resident, comes into Kylie's life in an unexpected way. The attraction is immediate and they begin a passionate affair. As Kylie plunges into her new relationship, Lea remains suspicious.

When Kylie discovers Maya's bizarre connection to the murders, she is confronted with a terrible choice: kill, or allow an innocent to die. Her choice will affect the lives of everyone in Verhoven.

If you crave shock value and being kept in the dark until the last possible moment, then this story is a must-read for you!

Everlong

Left with unresolved feelings over Maya Holworth's mysterious abandonment, Kylie Vinson returns to New York and becomes obsessed with delving into psychic phenomena. She is drawn to Sophie Brighton, who is experiencing a recurrent nightmare where a faceless woman is trying to escape an unforeseen terror. Sophie is convinced the woman is trying to reach out to her through an altered state of being and that both of their lives are in danger. It is only when Sophie physically acts out her nightmare, with frightening consequences, that Kylie uses her psychic abilities to gain insight into her dilemma.

To Kylie's astonishment, while under hypnosis, Sophie describes Holworth House in explicit detail. She knows of its century-old past of once being a state-appointed mental asylum, and of the fire that led to the deaths of many innocent lives.

Sophie is convinced her dream woman's fate exists within Holworth House. Kylie returns to Holworth House, and with the help of her longtime friend and the town's historian, a young woman's diary is discovered. The diary dates back to her commitment to the asylum because of her "unnatural love for another woman." Through the woman's passages, Kylie learns of extreme acts of physical and emotional cruelty suffered by the patients at the hands of a demented psychiatrist and his sadistic staff. Kylie believes the woman and Sophie share a common bond, and that they need to unleash Holworth House's dark secrets through "streaming." Only then, can Sophie be set free.

Limbo

The "Maya Holworth Trilogy" continues one year later. While investigating a lead on a missing person's case, former Sheriff now turned Detective Lea Carlson collapses on a New York City subway platform and lapses into an unexplained coma.

Alerted to the news, Kylie Vinson and Maya Holworth join forces in piecing together the events leading up to Lea's bizarre incident. Soon, Kylie discovers an unsettling connection between the recent missing person's case and a series of ritualistic murders that occurred five years previous. Even more startling is Maya's strong belief that Lucise, a supernatural archenemy from her past, is at the root of the murders.

Together, Kylie and Maya embark on a harrowing journey that challenges their supernatural strength and emotional willpower. They will endanger all they hold dear in waging war with Lucise in a fight to the finish for good to triumph over evil.

Diver's Blues

After a tragic event involving a student drowning, Dive Master Jaime Forest sails from the Florida Keys northward on a soul-searching mission. Midway through her voyage, Jaime finds herself face to face with another crisis. A baby seal, ensnared in fishing net, becomes severely injured when the netting tangles in Jaime's boat propeller.

Help arrives in the form of A.J. Norris, a young, attractive marine biologist who manages a nearby mammal stranding center in a small beach town. Once they transport the seal to safety, they tend to its life-threatening wounds. With the seal too weak for relocation to a larger rehab facility on the mainland, and with Jaime's boat now damaged, A.J. and Jaime find themselves temporarily stranded.

From the moment A.J. and Jaime meet, their attraction for each other is undeniable and intense. As the days unfold, they can no longer hide their desire and they become lovers. But Jaime's guilt over the tragic drowning incident prevents her from opening up to A.J. on an emotional level, which leaves A.J. frustrated.

In the midst of their turmoil, they learn a Category 2 hurricane is fast approaching the coastline and that evacuation is mandatory. Refusing to leave the seal they've fondly named Clementine, Jaime and A.J. hunker down to weather the storm. Will they survive, or will Jaime's soul-searching expedition end in yet another senseless tragedy?

Bringing Rainbow Stories to Life

Visit us at our website: www.flashpointpublications.com